Mr. Benjamin went over to the man Devon had picked out and whispered into his ear. The man glanced over at Devon with a masked expression, then excused himself from the game.

Devon watched him get up and cross the room. Pete was tall and lean, and moved with powerful ease. There was something in his uncle's eyes that Devon could relate to—a driving, restless hunger, and a spot of vulnerability.

I know this guy, Devon thought. *We're family!*

Uncle Pete looked Devon over, obviously sizing him up as well. "So you say you're my nephew." His voice was arctic, without a trace of welcome or interest.

"That's right." Devon looked him in the eye and reined in his sappy hopes. *I'm not home yet,* he thought.

WITHDRAWN

D1390415

Visit the Official Sweet Valley Web Site on the Internet at:

http://www.sweetvalley.com

TOO HOT
TO HANDLE

TOO HOT
TO HANDLE

Written by
Kate William

Created by
FRANCINE PASCAL

BANTAM BOOKS
NEW YORK · TORONTO · LONDON · SYDNEY · AUCKLAND

TOO HOT TO HANDLE
A BANTAM BOOK : 0 553 50623 4

Originally published in USA by Bantam Books

First publication in Great Britain

PRINTING HISTORY
Bantam edition published 1998

The trademarks "Sweet Valley" and "Sweet Valley High"
are owned by Francine Pascal and are used under license by
Bantam Books and Transworld Publishers Ltd.

Conceived by Francine Pascal

Produced by Daniel Weiss Associates, Inc,
33 West 17th Street, New York, NY 10011

All rights reserved.

Copyright © 1996 by Francine Pascal

Cover photo by Oliver Hunter

Cover photo of twins © 1994, 1995, 1996 Saban – All Rights Reserved.

Condition of Sale
This book is sold subject to the condition that it shall not,
by way of trade or otherwise, be lent, re-sold, hired out
or otherwise circulated without the publisher's prior consent
in any form of binding or cover other than that in which it is
published and without a similar condition including this
condition being imposed on the subsequent purchaser.

Bantam Books are published by Transworld Publishers Ltd,
61–63 Uxbridge Road, Ealing, London W5 5SA,
in Australia by Transworld Publishers (Australia) Pty Ltd,
15–25 Helles Avenue, Moorebank, NSW 2170,
and in New Zealand by Transworld Publishers (NZ) Ltd,
3 William Pickering Drive, Albany, Auckland.

Printed and bound in Great Britain by
Cox & Wyman Ltd, Reading, Berkshire.

To Johanna McNelis

633702
MORAY COUNCIL
Department of Technical
& Leisure Services
JCY

Chapter 1

Elizabeth Wakefield and her sister, Jessica, stood in the doorway of the kitchen, gaping at the scene before them.

"I don't believe it!" Elizabeth murmured.

Their older brother, Steven, was locked in a passionate kiss with Lila Fowler, the richest and snootiest girl at Sweet Valley High—who also happened to be Jessica's best friend. The couple seemed totally unaware of their astonished audience.

Steven, a student at nearby Sweet Valley University, had temporarily moved back home when he'd taken an internship position at the District Attorney's office. He planned to become a lawyer someday, and the experience of working with the D.A. would be extremely valuable to his future career.

1

Unfortunately, Steven's move had caused problems with his girlfriend, Billie Winkler, also a student at SVU. They'd shared an apartment off campus for some time, and had seemed perfectly suited for each other. But Billie had resented Steven's decision to move out for the semester and the fact that he hadn't even discussed it with her first. They'd broken up shortly before Steven had left.

Elizabeth and Jessica had looked forward to having Steven at home for the semester. But he had arrived looking miserable and depressed. Jessica had insisted a new romance would perk him right up and that he needed to start dating other girls immediately.

But watching him now, locked in Lila's arms, Elizabeth was very sure that this was not the right girl for him. *It's like a scene from a horrible soap opera,* she thought. *Except that it's real!*

Lila had recently suffered her own share of tragic heartaches. A week ago, a fire had nearly destroyed Fowler Crest, her family's twenty-room mansion in Sweet Valley's exclusive Hill section. Gasoline traces had been found all over the estate, proving that the fire had been caused by arson. Worst of all, Lila's parents were away on vacation, leaving her to face the disaster alone. Mr. and Mrs. Fowler were staying at a resort on a remote island where no one could reach them.

Elizabeth caught herself staring at Lila's arms, which were wrapped around Steven's neck like two flesh-toned snakes. *How creepy!* Elizabeth thought, shuddering. She felt terrible about what Lila was going through, but it didn't change her opinion about what was happening in front of her. Lila was totally wrong for Steven.

Elizabeth glanced at her twin, and their eyes met. Jessica exhaled slowly and forcefully, her nostrils flaring and her eyes glimmering. She looked angry enough to explode.

That's all we need now, Elizabeth thought wryly. *Hurricane Jessica!* If unleashed, her twin's sudden fury could easily turn the soap opera scene into a low-budget horror flick.

Elizabeth looped her arm through Jessica's and pulled her sister out of the kitchen.

"What?" Jessica hissed, shrugging her arm free.

Elizabeth raised her finger to her lips in a silencing gesture. "Upstairs," she whispered.

Lost in Steven's kiss, Lila could almost pretend there was nothing wrong with her life. Nothing mattered except his strong arms around her, his soft breath fanning her cheek. It seemed impossible that someone had set her house on fire, nearly killing her, or that someone was trying to frame her for the crime.

But eventually the kiss ended. And a heartbeat later, Lila's raging nightmare became real again. Her eyes filled with tears, blurring her vision as she gazed at Steven's ruggedly handsome face. If it weren't for him, she'd feel all alone. She had no one else.

Even her parents had deserted her. They were on a secluded island in the South Pacific, having a second honeymoon—*again*. Since they'd remarried earlier that year, they'd taken several so-called second honeymoons. Lila wasn't sure if this one was actually their fourth or their fifth. But what mattered was that she couldn't reach them when she needed them most. She knew she would've fallen apart without Steven.

Lila brushed her hands over his shoulders and along the top edge of his gray wool vest. "Tell me everything is going to be all right," she pleaded.

Steven kissed her forehead and held her close. "Everything *will* be all right," he assured her.

Lila closed her eyes and drew in a deep, shaky breath. She believed Steven and trusted him with all her heart. But feeling this special, warm thrill—especially with her best friend's older brother—had taken her totally by surprise. Lila had recently broken off her relationship with Bo Creighton, a gorgeous millionaire who lived in Washington, D.C. They'd met while working as junior counselors at a summer camp and had fallen instantly in love. Although she and Bo had tried hard to maintain their long-distance romance, the passion between them had eventually fizzled out and died.

A week ago, Lila had burned Bo's old letters and the mementos of all her dashed hopes. She had known their relationship wouldn't last forever, but the breakup had left her heartbroken just the same. Alone in the big mansion, Lila had cried herself to sleep on the divan in front of the fireplace. It was then that someone had tried to burn her house down around her.

Hours later, Lila had woken up in the hospital, her throat raw from the smoke she'd inhaled. She had opened her eyes slowly and, through a cloud of groggy pain, seen Steven's face. Since then, he'd become her knight in shining armor.

Lila pressed her lips against the side of his neck. *Steven is going to get to the bottom of this terrifying mystery and make me feel safe again*, she thought.

Steven stroked his hand through her long brown hair and whispered her name. Lila breathed a soft sigh and wrapped her arms around his lean, muscular back. Her heart pounding, she lost herself in another deep, searing kiss.

Jessica paced across her bedroom floor like a caged tiger, kicking her way through the piles of clothes and shopping bags strewn across the purple carpet. The image of Steven and Lila burned her mind's eye as though it were permanently branded into her brain. Jessica could picture them as clearly as if she were still in the kitchen: Lila's perfectly manicured fingernails resting against Steven's gray vest . . . Steven's hands on her waist . . .

"Calm down, Jess," Elizabeth said.

Jessica whirled around and glared at her sister. Elizabeth was sitting on the unmade bed with her back resting against the headboard, acting way too reasonable in light of what was going on downstairs at that very moment.

"I don't *want* to calm down," Jessica snapped. "Why did you drag me out of the kitchen?"

"Because you were ready to explode," Elizabeth responded smoothly.

Jessica clenched her fists and began pacing again. "I have every right to explode! Lila and I are so close, we're practically related," she said, grimacing. "It's like your brother going out with your cousin or something. And isn't that illegal?"

"But they're *not* cousins," Elizabeth pointed out.

Jessica crossed her arms. "So you *approve* of what they're doing?"

Elizabeth shook her head. "No, of course not," she answered. "They're totally wrong for each other. Steven's a burgers-and-baseball kind of guy, and Lila is caviar and the Concorde all the way." She shrugged. "I don't understand why they can't see it themselves."

Jessica exhaled sharply. "Because Steven and Lila are blind, or insane . . . or *both!*"

She grabbed one of the shopping bags and flung it across the room. "After all I did for that girl," she raged. "I tried so hard to cheer Lila up after the fire. I spent hours and hours putting together a beautiful photo album for her because she was so upset about losing her mementos. She lost her entire wardrobe, so I took her out on that huge, *exhausting* shopping spree. . . . Is this the thanks I get?"

Laughing, Elizabeth looked at the clothes piled around the room. "You haven't even given her the album yet, Jess. And your thanks is having all of Lila's new things here to borrow whenever you want," she said.

Jessica sneered at her. "Very funny, Liz. But while you're cracking jokes, Lila and Steven are downstairs, making a huge, disastrous, and totally disgusting mistake! We have to stop it!"

Elizabeth gave her an annoying know-it-all look. "We have to think this through logically, Jess," she insisted.

Jessica rolled her eyes. *Of course Ms. Logical would say that*, she thought hotly.

The twins were physically identical, with sleek, shoulder-length blond hair, blue-green eyes, and lean, athletic figures. But the similarities between them stopped at the surface. To Elizabeth, being logical was almost a hobby, along with being reasonable, sensible, serious—and totally *dull,* in Jessica's opinion. Elizabeth's whole life was neat and organized. She got straight A's in school, and spent much of her free time reading poetry or writing for the *Oracle,* Sweet Valley High's student newspaper. Her longtime boyfriend, Todd Wilkins, was one of the most boring guys at SVH, and her best friends, Enid Rollins and Maria Slater, weren't much better.

Jessica, on the other hand, believed in living each day to the fullest. Her world was full of bright colors and strong emotions. She loved crowds, especially if she was the center of attention. She was just as serious as Elizabeth about the things in life that really mattered, such as boys and shopping. Jessica was very sociable and enjoyed school for that reason, but she didn't believe in straining her brain on academics. She was satisfied to earn the minimum grade requirement to keep her position as cocaptain of the SVH cheerleading squad.

She was an action person, always on the lookout for excitement and adventure. When an idea popped into her head, she rarely wasted time planning out the details or worrying about unforeseen consequences. Both twins had strong personalities and placed high demands on themselves. But while her sister was more concerned with being *right*, Jessica put her energy into getting results. The idea of leaving Lila and Steven alone together in the kitchen gnawed at her.

"I think we should march down there and put a stop to it!" Jessica said.

"No," Elizabeth insisted. "It would only make things worse."

"How could things *get* any worse?" Jessica retorted. "Lila and Steven . . . at this very moment . . ." She shuddered. "It's revolting!"

"It certainly is . . . *strange*," Elizabeth said. "But we have to be careful. Steven and Lila are both incredibly headstrong. Outside pressure and disapproval might only push them closer together. We have to help them realize what a mistake they're making, without being obvious about it. They have to feel as if it's their own decision to break up."

Jessica chewed her bottom lip as she considered her sister's point. "Maybe you're right," she said. Steven had always been resistant to any help in his love life. Jessica recalled how angry he'd been when she tried to fix him up with her friend Cara Walker, even though, in the end, he and Cara had ended up together for some time.

They'd broken up only because Cara had moved to London.

"The fact that Steven and Lila are both on the rebound doesn't help matters either," Elizabeth added.

Jessica pushed a heap of silk blouses off the bed and plunked herself down next to her twin. "I guess we'll have to do it your way," she said. "Our brother is too stubborn to accept the fact that we know what's best for him, and if I know Lila, she isn't about to give him up until she's good and ready."

After driving all night, Devon Whitelaw reached the outskirts of St. Louis, Missouri, just before sunrise Saturday morning. The gas gauge on his Harley-Davidson motorcycle pointed straight at empty. Noticing it, Devon cracked a smile. He'd kept himself alert during the long, boring hours on the road by working math problems in his head. He'd calculated his average gas mileage, breaking it down as far as the number of yards traveled per pint of gasoline, and figuring the distance he could cover between fuel stops. So far, all of his estimates had been right on target.

Playing with numbers also helped him block out the painful memories that followed him like a gray, gloomy shadow. He'd collected quite a cache of them in his seventeen years. Some dated back to his childhood—faded images of strangers hired to raise him. His parents had been too wrapped up in their own lives to do the job themselves.

Devon clenched his jaw as a familiar, hollow ache settled in his heart. He'd grown up in a huge, lavish house in a wealthy Connecticut town, but it had never felt like a home.

Devon's parents had been killed recently in a car accident. He wished he could mourn for them, maybe shed a few tears, but their deaths had left him unaffected. His lips twisted in a humorless smile. *No surprise there,* he thought. He had learned at a young age to rely on no one but himself.

Devon had wanted to strike out on his own months ago, when he'd turned seventeen. But his parents had adamantly refused. They'd spouted some sappy words about family togetherness, but Devon hadn't been fooled. He knew the issue had more to do with control and power than anything resembling family togetherness.

But now Devon was finally on his own—almost.

Even in death, James Allan Whitelaw III had managed to keep his son on a leash. His will provided Devon with a twenty-million-dollar trust fund—and the stipulation that he live with a legal guardian until he reached twenty-one years of age.

Devon squeezed his fists tighter around the handlebars of the bike. *At least the old man is letting me pick my own guardian,* he thought. Devon would receive one half of his inheritance—ten million dollars—upon choosing a guardian. The other half would be released to him when he turned twenty-one.

The kids Devon had grown up with in Connecticut assumed he'd led a charmed life as a spoiled rich kid. Devon was tall and good-looking, which had automatically made him popular with the girls. But none of them had seen past his ruggedly handsome face or his deep slate blue eyes. No one had cared for the person inside the tough-guy mask. Nor had anyone ever guessed that Devon would have traded all of his wealth just to be part of a loving family.

Devon had thought he'd found the home he'd always dreamed of when he'd moved in with his cousins in Ohio just after his parents' death. Unfortunately, the idea of a ten-million-dollar windfall had turned the whole family into a pack of greedy parasites. His aunt and uncle had automatically assumed they would become his legal guardians.

Within hours of Devon's arrival, they had begun making plans to remodel their modest split-level home. Their two sons, Ross and Allan, had turned into whiny, spoiled brats. After staying with them for only one week, Devon had hit the road again. This time, he was headed for Las Vegas to search for his uncle Pete.

Devon took the next exit off the interstate and pulled into a truck stop. He took off his helmet and pushed his fingers through his thick brown hair. His legs felt stiff as he hoisted himself off the bike. Yawning deeply, he unzipped his black leather jacket and stretched his arms out wide. He grimaced at the heavy odor of gasoline and exhaust fumes that hung in the air.

Devon could barely keep his eyes open as he waited for his turn at the gas pumps. He realized the long hours on the road had finally caught up with him.

After he'd taken care of filling his gas tank, he cruised over to the adjacent motel. A large sign proclaimed it to be The Serenity Rest Stop.

Devon smirked. *Sounds more like a funeral parlor,* he thought as he ambled into the motel office. A slight, white-haired woman was sitting behind the front counter, reading a newspaper. She looked up and smiled.

"Good morning," she said cheerfully. "Looks like that storm they've been predicting might pass us by, don't you think?"

Feeling much too tired to chat about the

weather, Devon dispensed with the pleasantries.

"I want a room," he responded curtly.

"Been on the road all night?" she asked.

Devon pulled his wallet out of his back pocket and took out a credit card. "I want a single, non-smoking if possible." He slapped the card on the glass counter.

Just then the phone rang. The woman smiled apologetically at Devon as she answered it. "Serenity Rest, one moment please." She covered the mouthpiece and turned to Devon. "Help yourself to coffee," she whispered, pointing to the large urn and insulated paper cups set up on a side table. "I just made it fresh."

Devon drummed his fingers on the glass counter. He didn't want coffee, and he resented being made to wait. He glanced around the small office, noting the faded gold couch and chair, threadbare brown carpet, and tacky framed prints on the wall.

At last the clerk ended the call. "Sorry about that," she said. "Now, where were we?"

"I need a room," Devon stated flatly.

"Yes, of course." She processed his credit card and handed it back to him along with a registration form and a cheap plastic pen bearing the motel's logo. "How many nights are you planning to stay?" she asked.

Devon uncapped the pen. "No nights," he

replied. "I just want to get a few hours sleep. I'll be out of here by noon."

"Oh, dear," she said with a frown. "Check-in time isn't until one P.M. You might try the Holiday Inn at the next exit."

Devon exhaled wearily. He could hardly see straight from lack of sleep, and his legs felt ready to give out any minute.

"Listen, lady, I've been on the road since yesterday," he said. "If I thought I could make it as far as the next exit, I wouldn't have stopped at this dump in the first place. Either find me a room *now* or let me speak with the manager."

The woman glared at him, her blue eyes wide and suddenly fierce. "I don't know who you think you are, but you can just turn around and waltz yourself out of my motel," she shot back. "I don't rent rooms to spoiled brats like you."

Taken aback by her sharp scolding, Devon cringed. *I guess I deserved that,* he thought, kicking himself for acting like a total jerk. "I'm sorry," he told her. "I didn't mean to be so rude. It's just that I was up all night, and—"

"So was I," she snapped, cutting off his excuses.

Devon flinched and lowered his eyes. *The poor lady was only trying to be friendly and helpful. And I sure picked a nice way to thank her!* he chided himself.

15

He cleared his throat and glanced up at her. "I really am sorry," he said. He held his breath, waiting for her to reply, hoping she would accept his apology.

She gave him a long, pointed look, but said nothing.

Finally Devon lowered his eyes again. He felt a deep, empty sadness in his gut. Pushing his hands into the pockets of his jacket, he turned to go.

Just as he reached the door, the woman spoke. "The housekeeping staff comes in at six o'clock," she remarked softly.

Devon turned around and gave her a hopeful, questioning look.

"There might be a room available shortly after six, if you care to wait," she explained briskly.

Devon nodded. "I'll take it," he replied gratefully.

She gave him a long, measuring look. "Have a seat and I'll see what I can do."

Devon obeyed automatically and carried his pack over to the lumpy couch. A few minutes later, she brought him a warm corn muffin and a carton of orange juice.

"Thanks," Devon said, touched by the kind gesture.

The woman sniffed. "Try not to get crumbs all over the place."

"I won't," he promised meekly. He watched her walk back to her station behind the front desk. For some reason, the woman's no-nonsense glare and brusque manner made Devon feel like a five-year-old kid.

Devon chuckled as he suddenly realized why. She reminded him of Nan Johnstone, the nanny he'd had growing up.

A wistful feeling welled up inside him. Devon hadn't thought of Nana in years. She had been his favorite person in the whole world, even though one of her sharp looks could send him running for cover. She'd always had a way of knowing when he'd been up to mischief. Unlike the other adults in his life, she hadn't been easily fooled by an innocent expression or charmed by a dazzling smile.

Nana was the only person he could remember who would actually sit down and talk with him. Most afternoons, she'd pour him a glass of milk and herself a cup of tea, and they'd discuss whatever was on his mind at the time. She had been sitting in the audience when he'd won first place in the math tournament in second grade. On his birthday, she had baked cupcakes for his whole class.

Devon had often fantasized to himself that Nana was his real mom. *But she wasn't*, he reminded himself firmly.

Resentment shot through him, chasing away the fond memories. In the end, Nana had turned out to be just like the rest of the strangers that had passed through his life. She had left his parents' employment and Devon had never seen her again. She'd never even bothered to answer the many letters he'd written to her over the years.

Devon popped the last bite of the corn muffin into his mouth and chewed slowly. Too many times he'd been taken in by people who pretended to care about him for their own selfish reasons. His parents had wanted a dutiful son to enhance their social status. Nana had been paid wages to spend time with him. More recently, Uncle Mark and Aunt Peggy in Ohio had welcomed him into their home in order to get their hands on his money.

Devon crushed his empty juice carton. He vowed not to let it happen to him again. His days of being used were over forever.

Devon had no idea what to expect in Las Vegas. He wasn't even sure his uncle Pete still lived there. Pete had left home years ago and, except for a few sporadic Christmas cards, he hadn't kept in touch. Devon's grandfather had cut Pete out of his will for extreme bad-boy behavior. Family gossip had it that he was a card shark, a loan shark, and a shark with the ladies.

Devon smirked. He'd tried to find a home with people he'd thought were good and upstanding, and he'd been bitterly disappointed. Maybe he'd have better luck with the black sheep of the family.

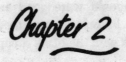

Chapter 2

Steven sat in his cubicle at the D.A.'s office, his insides twisted in knots. He'd come in early to review the file on the Fowler Crest case. The evidence against Lila was mounting, but Steven still had trouble believing that she could be the arsonist.

He found the computer printout that had been left on his desk the previous week. It was information taken from a Web page, a psychological profile of the typical arsonist. How it had gotten into his box was still a mystery. He'd asked everyone in the office, and no one claimed to have sent it. Adele, the receptionist who handled most of the busy office's mail and phone messages, had told Steven that it hadn't come through her.

Steven sat back in his chair and skimmed the

profile again: *An arsonist is crying out for help and attention . . . needs affection . . . looks for excitement . . . feels tension or emotional arousal before the act . . . is fascinated by fire paraphernalia.*

Steven closed his eyes and groaned. Lila fit the description all too well. She'd admitted to being distraught about her recent breakup with her boyfriend, and she certainly was the kind of girl who needed affection. *I'm just the kind of guy who doesn't mind providing it,* Steven thought wryly. Whenever he was around her lately, all of his professionalism and clear-thinking skills flew straight out of his mind.

Steven reached for his cup of coffee, next to the file. He took a sip, barely noticing that the liquid had grown cold. *Fascinated by fire paraphernalia,* he read again. He shook his head woefully. A few evenings ago, he and Lila had gone out to dinner to discuss her case. He recalled the fascinated look on her face as she stared at the flickering candle flame on their table. Then, as they left the restaurant, Lila had pocketed a book of matches. "To collect new memories," she'd explained.

That does make sense, Steven assured himself. After all, the fire at Fowler Crest had wiped out every single one of Lila's mementos. She'd wept over the loss of her photos and souvenirs, a lifetime of stored memories. *But why matches?* he wondered. There had also been a stack of postcards depicting the restaurant's interior. Lila could have just as easily taken one of them instead.

The case was turning out to be a labyrinth of clues—which all led to Lila Fowler.

Steven grabbed a pencil from the top drawer of his desk along with a yellow legal pad. He drew a thick line down the middle of the paper and wrote *G* and *NG* at the top of the columns: *G* for guilty, *NG* for not guilty. The list on the guilty side was easy. A gallon container of gasoline had been found in Lila's car. Steven himself had found a pair of gasoline-soaked gloves belonging to her at the scene of the crime. The Web page information added several more items.

Steven switched his attention to the other column. His fingers tightened around the pencil as he struggled to come up with evidence to prove Lila's innocence. She had mentioned having the feeling that someone was watching her and that someone had trespassed into Fowler Crest the evening Steven had found the incriminating gloves in the bushes. But all that was only her word. Then again, all the hard evidence against her was circumstantial. It was possible that someone had planted it all in an attempt to frame Lila for the crime.

Deep in thought, Steven jumped when the phone on his desk buzzed. He picked it up and blurted his name into the mouthpiece. The caller was his boss, Sweet Valley's D.A., Joe Garrison, summoning Steven to his office.

Steven hung up and exhaled a deep breath. He gathered up his papers and tossed the coffee cup into the trash. He knew his boss expected him to help pin the fire on Lila. But despite the evidence, Steven remained convinced of her innocence.

"I have a meeting with the mayor in twenty minutes," Joe Garrison explained as Steven entered his office. The D.A. ran a hand over his short, curly dark hair, then leaned back in his black leather chair and laced his fingers together behind his head. His wide black desk was cluttered with files and papers, as usual, and a stack of folders was piled precariously on the matching credenza behind him. "But before I go, I want an update on the Fowler case."

Steven pulled over one of the wooden chairs from along the wall and sat down across from his boss. "I thought I might take a closer look at the employee records for Fowler Industries," Steven said.

Mr. Garrison narrowed his deep blue eyes. "Why?"

Steven shifted uneasily. "I want to do a background check on everyone who's been fired or brought up on disciplinary charges."

"We have our suspect," Mr. Garrison said, shaking his head. "All we need now is motive. Without it, our case against Lila Fowler is weak. That's *your* job, remember?"

Steven nodded. "And I *have* been spending a lot of time with her, trying to get to know her, but . . ." He shrugged.

His boss leaned over the desk and glared at Steven. "You're supposed to be figuring out exactly why she set that fire," he barked. "What have you been doing instead?"

Steven felt his face grow hot. He imagined the scene with Lila in his kitchen Friday night and their heated kisses. *Lila is guilty of setting a fire all right— but not the kind you think,* Steven silently admitted.

Mr. Garrison picked up a pencil and tapped the eraser end on the desk. "Frankly, I'm disappointed, Steven. I expected high-quality work from you because I thought you were serious about this internship."

Steven flinched, as if he'd been socked in the jaw. "I've been doing exactly what you told me to do," he replied defensively. "I've been learning everything I can about Lila Fowler. I just don't think she's the kind of girl who would commit such a serious crime."

His boss began recounting the evidence against her, all of which Steven knew already. "An empty gas can was found in her car. And you yourself found her gas-soaked, monogrammed gloves in the bushes at her house."

Steven gulped. The evidence *did* point to Lila. *But I know she's innocent,* he reminded himself. "Anyone could have planted that evidence," he argued.

"What about the sulfur on her fingers after the fire?" Mr. Garrison asked. "Did someone plant that too?"

"Lila already explained that she was burning some letters in the fireplace that evening," Steven pointed out.

Mr. Garrison exhaled sharply. "Steven, this is an open-and-shut case." He spoke slowly, pronouncing each word clearly as if he were speaking to a not-so-bright child. "We work as a team in this office, and our goal is to put criminals behind bars. You can be part of the team, or you can leave right now."

Feeling totally defeated, Steven slumped in his seat. "I want to see the criminal punished," he said weakly.

"Then do your job!" Joe Garrison retorted, throwing up his hands. "We don't have time for wild-goose chases around here. The facts are what matter, and in this case, they point straight to Lila Fowler. She *is* guilty—and it's our job to prove it!"

Steven reluctantly admitted to himself that the evidence against Lila was overwhelming. *Is it possible that she really is guilty?* he wondered. *Am I fooling myself by believing in her innocence? Does kissing her make my head spin so fast, I can't see straight anymore?*

His boss gave him a suspicious look, as if Steven's thoughts were plastered across his forehead. "You don't have a, shall we say, *personal* interest in this case, do you, Wakefield?" Mr. Garrison questioned.

"Of course not," Steven responded cautiously.

Mr. Garrison raised his eyebrows. "It's already been established that Lila Fowler is a friend of your sister's, is she not?"

Steven's throat tightened as he realized he'd stepped into a trap. "Yes, but that doesn't mean—"

"And you have visited her home," Mr. Garrison interjected coolly.

"W-Well, yes . . . I've been, um, working on this case," Steven stammered.

His boss stood up and walked around the desk. Easily slipping into the role of interrogator, he leaned against the front of his desk and crossed his arms. "And before that. You've been to Fowler Crest for social occasions."

Under the glare of the District Attorney's piercing blue eyes, Steven felt like a specimen on a glass slide. "I went to her parents' wedding," he admitted.

"How would you rate Lila?" Mr. Garrison asked. "Aside from this case, do you think she's the kind of girl you might like to date?"

Steven squirmed uncomfortably. "I don't know," he hedged.

Mr. Garrison smirked. "But you wouldn't mind finding out, right?"

Steven swallowed hard. "OK, so Lila is a friend of my sister's and I've been to her house a few times. And I admit I think she's good-looking. That doesn't mean I can't be objective about the case."

"It might," Mr. Garrison told him. "You wouldn't be the first guy to get sucked in by a pretty face and sweet smile."

"That's not happening to me," Steven countered with a sinking feeling.

Mr. Garrison leaned closer. "Then what is?" he demanded.

"I just want to find the person who started that fire at Fowler Crest," Steven replied.

The D.A. gave him a hard look. "We *have*

found her, Wakefield. Now it's our job to see that justice is done."

How sickening! Jessica thought as she stared at Lila's dreamy expression during history class. She had a pretty good idea what—and *who*—was on her friend's mind at that moment. *How could Lila and Steven do this to me?* Jessica wondered.

Lila picked up her pen and began writing in her notebook, as if she were taking notes on Mr. Jaworski's boring lecture about the Louisiana Purchase. But Jessica leaned over and saw that Lila was merely drawing little hearts on the blank page. *I'm going to throw up,* Jessica thought.

Finally the bell rang, signaling the end of first period. As the students filed out through the door, Jessica grabbed Lila's arm.

"We have to talk, Li," she said as she pulled her friend into the empty classroom across the hall.

Lila tugged her arm free of Jessica's grasp and smoothed down the sleeve of her white cotton blouse. "What's wrong?" she asked.

Jessica slammed the door shut and whirled around to face Lila. "You and Steven," she hissed. "That's what's wrong!"

A wounded look flashed in Lila's brown eyes. She sank down into one of the desk chairs and folded her hands primly in her lap. Lila seemed extremely vulnerable, which was understandable considering all she'd been through recently.

Jessica caught her bottom lip between her teeth. She really did care about Lila. *Maybe I shouldn't be confronting her right now,* she thought. Then she recalled the image of Lila and Steven kissing in the kitchen, his hands spanning her waist, her arms curled around his neck . . .

Jessica shuddered, her stomach turning. Determined, she looked Lila in the eye and pressed on. "I thought you were my best friend, and here you are sneaking around with my brother!"

Lila raised her chin. "So? It's not a crime to go out with your best friend's brother."

Jessica perched on the corner of a desk and folded her arms. "That doesn't make it right," she countered. "And you know it. Otherwise you wouldn't have kept it a secret."

Lila shrugged. "I felt weird about telling you."

"That should tell you something," Jessica said. "Because I think what you're doing is plenty *weird!*"

Lila's expression hardened. "Maybe I didn't tell you about Steven because I knew you would react this way," she said. "And furthermore, I think your attitude stinks!"

"The problem isn't my attitude," Jessica retorted. "It's you and my brother."

Lila sniffed. "You didn't react this way when Steven was going out with Cara."

"Cara was different. She and Steven had a lot in common. She didn't live in a mansion. She lived in an apartment, and she . . ." Jessica drew a blank and let out an exasperated groan. "That has nothing to do with this," she said defensively. "You and Steven are completely wrong for each other."

"Thanks for your opinion," Lila spat. "But I don't happen to agree. And I have a strong feeling Steven wouldn't agree with you either."

Jessica exhaled wearily and moved to the chair next to her friend. "Lila, tell me the truth," she began, scooting closer. "Would you rather have a BMW kind of guy, or a VW one? Steven loves that junky yellow Bug he drives. He'll never give it up for a luxury car."

Lila smiled. "I don't mind."

"What about other things?" Jessica asked. "Do you want a guy who snacks on pâté and caviar, or on potato chips and onion dip?"

"I know what you're getting at," Lila said. "But Steven is a refreshing change from the guys I usually date. I feel like I can relax and be myself when I'm with him." She crossed her legs and laced her fingers on her knee. "Besides, he didn't do too badly when we went to Chez Costa.

I think oysters have become one of his favorite appetizers."

Jessica clenched her jaw. Chez Costa was a fancy French restaurant in downtown Sweet Valley, and definitely not her brother's style. "Steven wears mismatched socks, Lila. With *holes!*"

Lila giggled. "I know," she responded coyly. "We've gotten past the shoes-off stage."

Jessica shuddered, thoroughly grossed out. "You know that blue sweater he wears?" she persisted. She didn't enjoy putting down her own brother, but she reminded herself it was for his own good. "Steven bought that sweater at a yard sale," she told Lila. "And I've seen him eat cold chili straight out of the can."

Lila smiled dreamily. "That's kind of cute," she remarked.

Jessica's heart sank. With increasing desperation, she revealed more tidbits and secrets about Steven that she hoped would turn Lila off.

"Once I walked in on him and his friends having a burping contest," Jessica told her. "They were guzzling bottles of root beer to make themselves burp better. All of a sudden, Steven burst out laughing and brown foam came spewing out of his mouth and nose. He was declared the winner," she added dryly. "Is that the kind of guy you want in your life, Lila?"

Lila crossed her arms and pursed her lips. "Thanks for the advice and support, *friend*," she replied hotly. "But you just don't get it, do you? I'm going through a living nightmare. My house was burned down. I lost *everything*. At least Steven is there for me when I need him. Which is more than I can say for you right now."

Jessica's jaw dropped. "Just hold on one minute!" she shot back indignantly. "I have been there for you from the very beginning. Who was it that helped you put together a new wardrobe?"

Lila snorted. "I don't need new clothes right now. I need to feel safe."

Jessica ran her tongue over her teeth as she considered her words. "I'm sorry for what you're going through, Lila," she said truthfully. "And I want to be a friend who'll stand by you no matter what. But until you get over my brother, you can count me out."

"Fine!" Lila snarled as Jessica stormed out of the room. "I don't need you anyway!"

"Home, sweet home," Devon mumbled dryly as he drove north on U.S. highway 93 Tuesday evening. The neon lights of Las Vegas were up ahead, gleaming brilliantly in the night sky.

Thoroughly exhausted, Devon considered checking into a motel along the road. Although he'd stopped to rest during the grueling trip from Ohio, he'd rarely gotten more than two or three hours of sleep at a time.

His stomach growled, reminding him that he'd been living on vending machine food and sour coffee for days. The idea of a hot shower, some takeout Chinese food, and a night's sleep seemed incredibly appealing. He could wait until morning to start searching for his uncle.

But as Devon drew closer to the city, a restless feeling stirred inside him. He was tired of having his life strewn about in pieces, and longed to get things settled once and for all.

Of course, it would have been much easier if his father's will hadn't stipulated the part about having to find a guardian. Devon would have been overjoyed to make a cross-country trip and settle down anywhere that might appeal to him.

Devon pushed the thought out of his mind. *Face the facts,* he ordered himself. He had to live with a guardian for four more years. *I can handle that,* he thought. After all, he'd survived seventeen years with his parents in Connecticut.

Devon stopped at a gas station on the outskirts of town to fuel up and to check the oil in the motorcycle. He was surprised to see a bank of slot machines along the wall when he went inside to pay for his gas.

The clerk, a tall woman with a shaved scalp,

tattooed face, and silver chains looped from her ears to her lips, flashed him a big smile. "Try your luck, sugar?"

Devon shook his head—and tried not to stare at the dragon and bloody sword on her cheek. Then he caught a glimpse of himself in the glass counter and flinched at the gruesome reflection. His hair was sweaty and plastered down from his helmet. His chin was covered with dark stubble, and his blue eyes were glassy and unfocused. *I'm no prize either,* he thought, snickering.

Devon went out to the bike and retrieved his shaving kit. In the rest room, he splashed some cold water over his head, combed his hair, and shaved. "Not great, but at least not gruesome," he muttered as he inspected himself in the small mirror over the sink. His eyes were still bloodshot, with deep circles around them. But shaving the dark shadows off his angular features made him appear a hundred times more respectable.

Devon shrugged on his black leather jacket and gathered his things. He returned to the bald clerk and bought a street map of Las Vegas. At the telephone booth in the parking lot, he searched through the phone book for his uncle's name. He didn't find it.

Devon dropped the directory, letting it dangle at the end of its chain. He'd planned on finding his uncle's address and just showing up at the door. *What if he doesn't even live here anymore?* Devon worried. He'd found a Christmas card from Pete dated years earlier in his father's desk. The envelope had been postmarked from Las Vegas, Devon's only clue to his uncle's whereabouts.

Devon chewed the corner of his lip as he considered his next step. It was possible that his uncle lived in Vegas but didn't have a phone or didn't have a listed number. Seizing on that hope, Devon quickly picked up the receiver and called directory assistance.

"I'm sorry, the number for Peter Whitelaw is unpublished," the operator told Devon, confirming his theory.

Devon hung up and ambled back to his bike. He felt frustrated but hopeful. At least he knew his uncle was still in Las Vegas . . . *somewhere*.

"I'll just have to comb the entire city," Devon muttered under his breath as he started the engine. He decided to check out the casinos, one by one. Filled with newfound determination and energy, Devon roared out of the parking lot.

Within minutes, he was cruising along Las Vegas Boulevard, which was commonly known as the Strip. All around him, lights swirled and pulsed in a dazzling array. Tubes of colorful neon lights flashed the names of the casinos and hotels. Marquees flaunted their big-star entertainment.

This is a carnival! Devon thought, gawking at the sights. Las Vegas hardly seemed like a place where real people lived.

Devon left his motorcycle in a parking garage and hit the pavement on foot. After five days on the road, it felt great to be walking.

The first casino on Devon's route was the Luxor Hotel. The building was shaped like a pyramid, with giant cats at the entrance, all ablaze in neon colors. A huge spotlight blazed upward from the peak.

The interior of the casino was decorated in shades of orange, blue, and gold. Devon's gaze moved slowly across the large, open area. The air was charged with excitement, punctuated by the occasional clanking noise of coins dropping from the slot machines.

Devon made his way over to the bar and ordered himself a glass of club soda. "I'm looking for a guy named Pete Whitelaw," Devon told the bartender.

The man's expression remained bland as he pulled a hose from under the bar with one hand

and scooped up a glass full of ice with the other. He aimed the nozzle and filled the glass with club soda. "Wish I could help you," he said, adding a twist of lemon to the drink.

Devon paid for the soda, adding a ten-dollar tip. "I don't suppose Pete comes in here occasionally, does he?"

The bartender pocketed the money. "Occasionally, maybe."

Devon plunked another ten-dollar bill on the bar.

The man eyed it suspiciously before picking it up. "Is Pete in trouble again?"

Devon flinched. *In trouble again?* he repeated silently, wondering just what kind of trouble Pete was known for being in. "I'm his nephew," he told the bartender. "I'm looking for him about a . . . family matter."

The man nodded. "If I see him around, I'll let him know."

At the Excalibur Hotel, across the street, Devon questioned a dealer at one of the gaming tables. A woman sitting at the table burst out laughing. "That snake is your uncle?"

Devon turned to her. Dressed in red spandex and tons of jewelry, she could have just as easily been in her early twenties as in her late fifties. It was hard to tell with all the makeup plastered on her face. "Do you know where I can find him?" he asked her.

"I wish I did," she said, her voice slurred. "I'm looking for him myself."

"When's the last time you saw him?" Devon asked, his hopes rising. "Do you have his address?"

She laughed again. "Pete is a very slippery man."

Devon rubbed his hand over his chin. "That's the picture I'm getting too."

The woman leaned back and gave Devon an intense, up-and-down stare. "You're a hunk," she said.

Devon cracked up at that. *This place is so bizarre!* he thought.

The woman winked her fake eyelashes at him. "Honey, you tell that snake uncle of yours that Della is looking for him too," she said. "And I'm still waiting for the five hundred he owes me!"

"Great," Devon muttered sarcastically under his breath as he walked away. Clearly the image he'd formed of his uncle was right on target. *The man sure seems to be earning his title of black sheep of the Whitelaw clan,* Devon thought.

Hours later, Devon felt ready to give up for the night. He was dizzy from hunger and lack of sleep, and he felt as if his head were spinning like a top.

He staggered into the front lobby of the Starscape Hotel, barely able to focus his eyes.

This is the last one, he decided. Devon promised himself a hot meal and a motel room for the night after he'd checked out the Starscape.

Devon asked one of the waitresses in the casino if she knew his uncle. The woman gave him a non-committal smile and told him to wait.

A moment later, a man wearing a blue velvet jacket came over to him. "I'm Mr. Benjamin, the floor manager," he told Devon. "Would you mind stepping into my office?"

Devon eyed him warily. *Did I break a law or something?* he wondered. *Or is Uncle Pete so bad that anyone looking for him automatically gets in trouble?*

Keeping his thoughts to himself, Devon shrugged and dragged himself to his feet. "Sure, why not?" he mumbled, silently adding, *I've come this far already.*

Devon followed the manager through a service hallway. Unlike the glitzy decor of the public areas, this part of the casino was scaled down to plain drab. The walls were painted muted beige and the floor was covered with brown utility-grade carpet.

Mr. Benjamin ushered Devon into a small, cluttered office and sat down behind the green lacquered desk. "Have a seat," he said, gesturing to the cushioned chair in front of the desk.

Devon sat down cautiously. He felt the same way he had when he'd been sent to the principal's office in second grade for lifting his teacher's wig from her head while she was kneeling down. "What's this all about?" he asked defensively. "I was only checking around to see if anyone knew my uncle."

"Here at the Starscape Hotel, we take pride in making our customers feel at home," the manager replied. "Security is important to us. Many of our patrons are celebrities or prominent members of the business community."

Devon sighed wearily. It seemed his search for Uncle Pete would be a lot harder than he'd thought. "Listen, I really wasn't trying to make anyone nervous. I'm just trying to find my uncle."

"I see," Mr. Benjamin murmured. "Is your uncle employed at the Starscape?"

Devon shrugged. "I have no idea."

"I see," Mr. Benjamin murmured again. "You're looking for an uncle but you have no idea . . ." He stopped and folded his hands on the desk. "Describe this uncle of yours."

"I can't," Devon admitted.

Mr. Benjamin nodded slowly. "I see."

Devon exhaled a gust of breath. "I know this sounds totally suspicious, but I'm telling you the truth. My name is Devon Whitelaw and I'm looking for my uncle, Pete Whitelaw, who I'm sure lives in Las Vegas."

"Would you mind stepping into the waiting room for a moment?" Mr. Benjamin asked abruptly.

Devon rolled his eyes but complied with the man's request.

In the outer office, Devon sprawled out on one of the leather couches. He could hear Mr. Benjamin on the phone but couldn't make out the words. *Is he going to have me arrested for trying to find Pete?* Devon wondered. He was too tired and discouraged to care anymore, and wished he'd postponed his search until morning.

A few minutes later, the manager came out of his office. Devon sat up straighter and looked at him expectantly.

"Let's go," Mr. Benjamin said brusquely.

"Where?" Devon asked, his heart pounding suddenly.

Mr. Benjamin held the door open for Devon, then locked it behind them. "To the eleventh floor," he answered.

Devon blinked. Suddenly the mysterious treatment made sense. Pete was probably a regular patron at the Starscape, and everyone had been trying to protect his privacy. *I found my uncle!* Devon thought hopefully.

They rode upstairs in a private elevator. Devon felt excited and nervous as he was ushered into a small but lavish room. A bar was set up along the wall, and a bartender and two waiters stood unobtrusively to the side. *This must be where the high rollers play,* Devon presumed.

Three women and five men were seated around a table, playing blackjack. Almost afraid to look, Devon forced himself to study their faces. His gaze went immediately to the man sitting next to the dealer. The guy had a strong, square jaw, cleft chin, and brown wavy hair. There was a serious glint in his slate blue eyes as he stared at the cards in front of him. *That's my uncle!* Devon thought, amazed at the family resemblance.

In the next instant, his guess was confirmed. Mr. Benjamin went over to the man Devon had picked out and whispered into his ear. The man glanced over at Devon with a masked expression, then excused himself from the game.

Devon watched him get up and cross the room. Pete was tall and lean, and moved with powerful ease. There was something in his uncle's eyes that Devon could relate to—a driving, restless hunger, and a spot of vulnerability.

I know this guy, Devon thought. *We're family!*

Uncle Pete looked Devon over, obviously sizing him up as well. "So you say you're my nephew." His voice was arctic, without a trace of welcome or interest.

"That's right." Devon looked him in the eye and reined in his sappy hopes. *I'm not home yet,* he thought.

Chapter 3

Devon's stomach rumbled hungrily as he looked over the menu in the casino restaurant. "The steaks are pretty good here," Pete offered. "But I'd stay away from the seafood. Chef K.C. Rae is on duty this evening."

Devon glanced at his uncle over the top of the menu. "What does that mean?"

Wearing a pin-striped silk suit, diamond cufflinks, and a gold watch, Pete blended in well with the glitzy Las Vegas atmosphere. "K.C. is a great cook, but she has no sense of timing when it comes to fish. She'll serve it up with raw slime in the middle or as dry as an old sponge."

Devon chuckled. "I take it you eat here often."

"I get comped for dinner and shows in most of the casinos on the Strip," he replied. He raised his glass and signaled a nearby waiter for a refill.

"Comped?" Devon asked, bemused.

Pete shrugged. "As in complimentary. It's part of the game in Las Vegas. The casinos make most of their revenue from gambling, and each person who walks in the door is a potential gambler—but only while they're in the building. So the management does everything possible to keep that person from leaving, especially if he or she is a regular customer. A smart player can get all the complimentary meals and free show tickets he wants."

Devon nodded thoughtfully. Clearly his uncle was just that—a smart player.

A waiter brought Pete another drink and took their orders. Following his uncle's advice, Devon ordered a steak.

"I'm sorry about your parents, kid," Pete said gruffly after the waiter left. "How did you know where to find me?"

"Family gossip," Devon replied.

His uncle laughed, but there was no humor in his eyes. "Great answer. I can almost believe you're my long-lost nephew." He raised his glass to Devon, then took a long drink.

"I *am* your nephew," Devon insisted.

Uncle Pete narrowed his eyes. "What college did your father and grandfather graduate from?" he asked in a challenging tone.

"Yale," Devon answered smoothly. "My mother went to Smith."

Pete downed the rest of his drink. "What was your grandfather's nickname?"

Devon glanced away as he considered the question. He thought back to when his grandfather Whitelaw was alive, but couldn't remember any mention of a nickname. "I don't know," he admitted finally.

Uncle Pete smirked. "OK, next question. Let's see . . . where did your parents meet?"

"In Newport," Devon replied. "At a party or something."

"It was at the yacht club," his uncle clarified.

Devon shrugged. "That's close enough." He was beginning to enjoy the contest.

The interrogation continued as their dinner was served. "Where did the Whitelaws come from?" Pete asked. He handed his empty glass to the waiter and told him to make it a double.

Devon's mouth watered as he cut a piece of meat and speared it with his fork. "England," he answered.

Pete pursed his lips and nodded. He'd also ordered a steak, but he made no move to eat.

"The Whitelaws settled in Virginia, but moved to Connecticut just before the Civil War," Devon continued. He took a roll from the breadbasket and slathered it with butter. "My father's great-grandfather was an abolitionist, so he moved his family and his business to the North."

Uncle Pete sniggered. "That's what they told you, huh?"

Devon swallowed the last of the roll and reached for another. "Isn't it true?"

Pete's blue eyes twinkled with a cold glint. "The old man was an enterprising opportunist who followed the scent of money. He made a quick fortune selling substandard equipment to the U.S. military."

Amazed, Devon stopped chewing. His father had drilled him on the noble honor of the Whitelaw family since Devon was a toddler.

"I'll bet no one told you that the Whitelaw fortune more than tripled during Prohibition," Pete said.

Devon shook his head. "Bootlegging?"

"And other nasty things," Pete replied.

"Like what?" Devon asked, intrigued.

Pete swirled the amber liquid in his glass. The ice made a tinkling sound. "Blackmail, for one. My grandfather owned several warehouses that he rented to bootleggers for exorbitant fees . . . and they had to keep paying even if they decided to quit the business. Otherwise, they'd end up in jail." He raised his eyebrows and gave Devon a sharp look. "You don't believe me?" he asked.

Devon sat back and stared at him. "It's such a wild contrast to everything I've been told."

Pete grinned knowingly. "I was fed the same squeaky-clean version as a kid. It wasn't until I did my own digging into the family records that I discovered the whole truth. Believe me, I was just as shocked as you are." He chuckled. "I felt like a kid who'd just found out there's no such thing as Santa Claus."

Devon gritted his teeth as an unbidden memory flashed across his mind. For years he had woken up on Christmas morning filled with childish hope. Then he'd see the limp, empty stocking he'd hung over the fireplace the night before, and his heart would break. Devon had tried leaving cookies out to bribe Santa. One year, he'd gone so far as to leave celery and lettuce for the reindeer. But always, his pathetic offerings would still be there in the morning, exactly as he'd left them.

Except when Nana was around, Devon reminded himself. Holidays had been special when Nan Johnstone had worked for the Whitelaws. Devon thought back to those few Christmas mornings when he'd found the cookies gone and his stocking stuffed with candy and silly trinkets. *Then Nana took off, and I grew up,* he thought bitterly.

Devon stabbed a chunk of his baked potato with his fork. "I never believed in Santa Claus," he said.

"Then you're smarter than I was," his uncle replied. He raised his glass for a toast, then frowned. "You need a *real* drink."

Devon snorted. "Maybe in a few years. I'm only seventeen."

"You look older," Pete remarked.

"Well, my driver's license doesn't," Devon remarked. "It says I'm seventeen."

"I'm afraid that won't do. The minimum age for casino gambling is twenty-one," his uncle told him. "We'll have to get you a new ID."

Devon eyed him narrowly. "Isn't that illegal?"

Pete nodded. "Yes, it is. And it truly pains me to break the law, but I have an obligation to uphold the Whitelaw tradition—and so do you, kid."

They both laughed uproariously. Then Pete raised his glass and called for a toast. "To the old skeletons in the Whitelaw closet . . . may you and I join them someday."

Devon picked up his water goblet and clinked glasses with his uncle. "Does that mean you believe I'm your nephew?" he asked.

"I knew it as soon as I saw you," Pete admitted. "Looking at you, I could be looking in the mirror twenty-five years ago. But I wasn't sure I'd like you. And when's the last time you had a shower, anyway? I understand you've been on the road, but if you're going to hang around me, you've got to wash."

Devon laughed. There was a harsh honesty about his uncle that struck a chord with him. "No problem," he replied. "Believe me, I'd love a shower."

Pete pushed aside his plate. "I've got three bathrooms and lots of space in my apartment," he told Devon. "You're more than welcome to stay."

Devon saw the sincerity in his uncle's expression and heard the vulnerability in his voice. Devon understood *that*. He'd learned early on that every invitation carried the risk of rejection.

Maybe I should tell Pete the whole truth about why I'm here, Devon thought. Then he remembered what had happened in Ohio. "I'd really appreciate it," he began hesitantly. "The only problem is, my parents left me broke." He hated lying to his uncle, but he wasn't about to make the same mistake he'd made with his aunt Peggy and uncle Mark.

"That's nothing," Pete replied, waving it off as if he were swatting a pesky fly. "I never needed the family or their money. And neither do you."

Devon felt a stirring of faith in this guy. "Are

you sure you don't mind if I crash with you for a while?"

"For as long as you want," his uncle insisted. "The disinherited bad apples that fell off the Whitelaw tree have to stick together."

Devon raised his eyebrows. "Even though I can't pay my share?"

Pete let out a derisive laugh. "I wouldn't take Whitelaw money anyway," he retorted. "I've done fine without it, and I'm *still* doing fine."

More than fine, Devon thought as he glanced at his uncle's gold watch and diamond cufflinks. Devon's money had triggered the Wilsons' greed, but maybe things would be different this time.

"By the way, what *was* Grandfather's nickname?" Devon asked, suddenly remembering the question that had stumped him earlier.

Pete tipped his head back and laughed. "That was a trick question," he replied, his voice somewhat slurred. "He didn't have one. Nobody ever called my father anything but Mr. Whitelaw. If you were very close to him, you called him *sir*. Even my mother called him that."

Devon sneered. "Sounds like my father."

"You got that right!" Pete said. "James Allan Whitelaw the Third was the old man's clone. Sometimes I thought—" He stopped abruptly and stared at something behind Devon.

Bemused, Devon looked over his shoulder to see what had caused his uncle's sudden reaction. A tall, elegant woman with long dark hair and brown eyes was being seated at the next table. She was beautiful, but not enough to startle a man like Pete.

Devon turned back to his uncle and watched him remove a thick wad of cash from his inside pocket. "Come on, let's get out of here," he said tersely as he scattered a few bills on the table.

"Sure," Devon murmured, thoroughly puzzled.

As they walked past the woman's table, Devon noticed her and Pete exchange a long glance. It was obvious they knew each other. *So why doesn't he say something to her?* Devon wondered.

Steven wrapped his arms tighter around Lila and brushed his lips against her forehead. They were snuggled together on the small couch in the Fowlers' pool house. Through the glass panels that ran the entire length of the far wall, Steven could see the water of the swimming pool shimmering in the moonlight. Lila had set up a temporary home for herself in the pool house while Fowler Crest was being repaired.

"I wish we could stay like this forever," Lila whispered. "You make me feel so safe."

Steven sighed. Lila's comment reminded him of

his reason for coming to see her that evening. Reluctantly, he pulled himself out of her embrace and rubbed his hand over his chin.

"What's wrong?" Lila asked in a little, frightened voice that tugged at his heart.

He smiled tenderly and pushed a lock of her brown hair behind her ear. "We're not going to make much progress on our case this way."

"You're absolutely right." She leaned back, resting her head on the cushioned arm of the couch and crossing her ankles on Steven's knee. "OK, time for work," she said. "Let's hurry and get it over with so we can get back to the important stuff," she added with a giggle.

Steven reached down and picked up the yellow legal pad and pencil that had fallen to the floor hours ago. "We need a list of suspects to work from." He wrote the word *suspects* across the top of the page and turned to Lila. "Do you have any enemies?" he asked. "Anyone who might want to get back at you for something?"

Lila tucked her hands behind her head. "I don't know . . . ," she began. "I suppose Della Luree would fall into that category. She was a maid I recently had to fire."

Steven took down the name. "What happened?"

"I caught her trying on my new Pierre Jové

satin tunic!" Lila exclaimed. "Of course she went to my parents and complained that I wasn't being fair."

"Anyone else?" Steven asked.

Lila pressed her lips together as she thought. "Greta Davis. She used to fill in on the cook's days off."

"Did you fire her too?" Steven asked.

"Not really," Lila replied. "But the food she prepared was ghastly and I refused to eat it. There was another cook a while back too. He couldn't make anything without dumping in at least a ton of butter or bacon fat. It was either fire him or turn into a blimp."

Steven chuckled. "You'd still look adorable," he teased, leaning over to give her a brief kiss.

Lila mentioned nearly a dozen more people who'd worked at Fowler Crest and whom she'd recently fired. "I think that's it for the domestic help," she said finally.

Steven nodded encouragingly and turned to a blank page. "Can you think of anyone else?"

Lila sighed. "Well, Joan Borden might still hold a grudge against me. She nearly tricked my father into marrying her. This was some time ago, before my parents got back together," Lila explained.

"Joan Borden," Steven repeated as he jotted down the name. "Do you think she blames you for breaking up her romance with your father?"

"I did," Lila replied matter-of-factly.

Steven gave her an incredulous look. "Would you care to elaborate?"

Lila propped herself up with her elbows. "Joan pretended to be a rich socialite from Los Angeles, but I wasn't fooled. Just before the ceremony began, I got her to admit that she was marrying my father to get her hands on his money . . . and her confession was overheard."

"Overheard by whom?" Steven prompted.

Lila smiled mischievously. "By everyone. One of the microphones for the sound system happened to be hidden in the bridal party's dressing room."

Steven's jaw dropped, then he burst out laughing. "Lila, you're something else."

Lila sniffed indignantly. "I had to protect my father from that greedy parasite. She also had a daughter who was equally as bad. Just the thought of having Jacqueline for a stepsister makes my skin crawl."

"This is a great lead," Steven said as he added another page of information to his notes. "I'm going to check this woman out first thing tomorrow morning. We'll see if she's made any recent trips to Sweet Valley. . . ."

Lila leaned toward him and draped her arms

over his shoulders. "Does that mean we're finished working?" she asked.

Steven moved back and shook his head. "Not quite. Let's go over a few more local suspects. Kids at school?"

Lila scowled playfully. "There are a few students at SVH who don't like me. Enid Rollins, Bruce Patman . . ."

Steven struggled to keep up as she continued reciting names. "What about old boyfriends?" he asked.

Lila moved closer and kissed him. "I can't remember any of them when you're around," she whispered.

Steven laughed. "Try," he said jokingly. "Even guys you may have dated once or twice on a casual basis."

Lila rolled her eyes. "I feel like I'm being interviewed for *Celebrity Insight* magazine," she muttered. "OK, the guys in my past . . . you already know about Bo," she pointed out. "I also went out with John Pfeifer, and with Tony Alimenti. And Mark Steward, a guy whose parents own a computer company in Oregon, took me sailing when both our families were vacationing in the Caribbean."

Steven put down the pencil and flexed his fingers, grimacing as if he were suffering an acute case of writer's cramp. "Now, out of these thousands of enemies and old boyfriends . . . ," he teased, then ducked as Lila threw a couch pillow at his head.

"Seriously, though, it is an impressive list," Steven told her. "We have five pages of suspects."

Lila shrugged. "I can't help it," she said. "Lots of people are just jealous of me."

"Who can blame them?" Steven teased, punctuating his question with a soft kiss. "This is very important, Lila," he said, looking her straight in the eye. "I want you to think very carefully. Out of all these names you've come up with, is there any one person who you believe is truly vicious—or crazy? Someone who wouldn't hesitate to hurt you physically, who you suspect is capable of violence?"

Lila sat back, her expression suddenly grave and her eyes wide with fear. A dark shadow seemed to pass across her face. Steven reached for her hands. They were ice cold.

Steven gulped, stunned by her strong reaction. Then his heart began to thump excitedly. *There* is *someone,* he realized. *Lila has a lead!* Whoever it was, she was obviously frightened just thinking about that person.

"What is it?" Steven whispered. "*Who* is it?"

Lila shook her head, avoiding his eyes. "Nothing," she mumbled.

Steven stroked his fingers through her hair, then cupped her chin in his hands and gently turned her toward him. "Lila, tell me."

"Home at last," Pete said as he ushered Devon into his swanky Las Vegas apartment. "There's plenty of room, so make yourself at home."

Devon followed his uncle through the high-ceilinged foyer, down a short flight of steps, and into an expansive, sunken living room. A highly polished black wet bar stood over to the left. In the center of the room, a black leather couch and two leather chairs formed a seating arrangement around a glass coffee table. Two brass bookcases flanked the sliding glass doors on the far wall. Devon noticed a small, very expensive stereo system on one of the shelves, with its speakers mounted discreetly near the ceiling.

"Not too shabby for you, I hope," Pete joked.

"I'll let you know," Devon replied in kind.

Pete laughed. "Spoken like a true New England snob," he teased. "Try to make yourself comfortable anyway, kid. I've got a few calls to make."

Left alone, Devon walked over to the sliding doors and stepped out onto the balcony. The building was located on Las Vegas Boulevard, right on the Strip. From his vantage point on the twenty-first floor, Devon could see the bright neon lights of the city flashing for attention like hawkers at a country carnival.

Well, it's not Connecticut, he thought, recalling the suburban luxury of his parents' home. *And it's not Ohio.* Devon had longed for something different, and it seemed he had it now.

A few minutes later, his uncle joined him on the balcony. "What do you think of my city?" he asked Devon.

"We sure seem to like our neon around here," Devon remarked drolly.

"That's part of the charm, kid." Pete leaned forward, bracing his elbows on the wrought-iron railing. "You're looking at the best place in the world to make your mark." He chuckled. "In fact, everywhere you look, there's a mark just waiting to be made, if you know what I mean."

Devon frowned. *Does that mean Pete is doing so well in Las Vegas because he cheats people?* he wondered.

"They say there's a sucker born every minute," his uncle continued. "But it's twice a minute in Vegas."

Devon glanced sideways at him. "Like those people you were playing cards with in that private room at the casino?" he asked pointedly. "Were they your *marks?*"

Pete gave him a long, hard look. "Don't like me taking advantage of the little people, huh? Well, don't worry. I'm just a master card player. Got this little calculator in my head."

Devon relaxed. "I know about that," he said. "It must run in the family. I've gotten straight A's in math and science my whole life."

Pete affectionately punched Devon's shoulder. "I think I could get used to having you around, kid. Even if you are family," he added jokingly.

Devon smiled.

"Cheating in the casinos is totally out of the question," Pete explained. "The gaming tables are monitored by discreet little cameras that are planted all over the place—a system we call 'the eye in the sky.' But it doesn't matter. Las Vegas is still a gold mine for people like us."

"How so?" Devon wondered aloud.

Pete gestured with a sweep of his hand. "Everything has been carefully staged to pull in the average sap and convince him to loosen his purse strings. The bright lights make him feel adventurous, totally different from the man he is in his normal, boring life. Most of the restaurants in the casinos offer simple, inexpensive dishes, like meat loaf and roast turkey, so Mr. Average won't feel intimidated. They work hard to make him feel comfortable, confident, and powerful—because that's when he's likely to pour out his money."

Devon listened, fascinated.

"A smart guy like you can use all that to his own advantage," Pete told Devon. "You can make a fortune by developing winning instincts. And once your luck hits and you win a few bucks, there are plenty of places where you can have fun spending it."

Devon ran his thumb along a ridge in the scalloped pattern of the railing. "If I do make money, I'll pay my share of the rent—help out with expenses at least," he said.

Pete laughed. "I told you, I don't need a dime of Whitelaw money—even from you. I have everything I want." His expression suddenly turned serious and a clouded look came into his eyes. "Everything a guy could ever want," he whispered tightly.

Devon stared at his uncle's profile. Something was obviously bothering Pete, but Devon didn't want to pry.

Pete glanced at him. "You don't believe me?"

Devon shrugged awkwardly and said nothing.

Pete gazed out at the neon horizon. "Yeah, kid, I've got it all." He paused. "Except for one thing."

"What's that?" Devon asked, curious.

Pete exhaled wearily. "A woman, what else?"

Devon raised his eyebrows, surprised. His uncle seemed incredibly smooth, sharp, and self-confident—hardly the type of guy Devon thought would have trouble with women.

"Hard to believe?" Pete asked, as if he'd read Devon's thoughts.

Devon nodded. "Yeah, sort of."

Pete sniggered. "Hard for me to believe it myself. I've always been a free spirit—until I met Linda. She and I even talked about getting married. But I lost her."

Devon was astonished to see this softer, vulnerable side of his uncle. Apparently Pete Whitelaw wasn't the hardened, selfish creature the family gossip had led him to believe. "What happened?" Devon asked.

Pete rubbed his hand over his chin. "She wanted a commitment, but I didn't want anything to change . . . so she dumped me," he muttered. "Same old story. It's a cliché. Comedians do stand-up routines about this stuff in the clubs. But it's not funny when it happens to you."

"I'm really sorry," Devon said.

Pete gave him a crooked smile. "Thanks, kid. So am I. Linda is something else. Dark hair, big brown eyes, long, gorgeous legs . . . she was in the restaurant tonight."

Devon nodded, remembering the woman at the adjacent table who'd caught his uncle's attention. "Yeah, I know who you mean."

"Seeing her tonight nearly killed me," Pete said. "I guess I never knew what I had until I lost her. But it was bound to happen," he said. "Linda Clark is a class act, and I'm—well, I'm the kind of guy I am . . . old-fashioned and rough around the edges. She would probably go for a guy more like you."

"What do you mean?" Devon asked.

Pete shrugged. "Linda needs a guy who's refined, one of those modern, sensitive types."

Devon raised his eyebrows. "That's what you think I am?"

"And I'm right too!" his uncle said, slanting him a teasing grin. "But don't you go getting any ideas about Linda, or I'll bust your chops!"

They both laughed. Devon raised his hands in mock surrender. "Don't worry, I'll stay miles away from her," he promised.

Uncle Pete gazed off into the distance. "I have a better idea," he said softly. "Maybe you can help me get her back."

Lila sat perfectly still as Steven's eyes held her pinned under their watchful stare. "Anyone on that list could have sneaked into Fowler Crest and started the fire," she insisted.

63

Steven gently brushed her hair back with his fingers. "Lila, there *is* someone you suspect, though, isn't there? Someone who you're sure is capable of violence."

Lila's chin trembled. Steven was right . . . there was one person. She pressed her bottom lip between her teeth and squeezed her eyes shut as she tried to push back the terrible memory that hovered at the edge of her mind. She didn't want to drag it out into the open. "No," she whispered, shaking her head. "I don't know anyone. . . ."

Steven wrapped his arms around her. "Please tell me," he prodded. "Help me find the person who destroyed your home."

Lila drew in a shaky breath and let it out slowly. "There is one person," she began. "A guy who . . . um, did get violent."

"Who?" Steven asked.

Lila swallowed hard. "John Pfeifer has been known to get rough on occasion."

Steven glanced at his notes. "One of the guys you went out with," he said, nodding.

Lila shrugged, hoping to cover up the churning emotions inside her. "John Pfeifer is a nobody."

"Did he ever get rough with you?" Steven asked.

"Maybe . . ." Lila nervously ran her tongue over the back of her teeth. "It was no big deal," she lied.

64

"Let me decide that," Steven said. "What happened?"

"It was nothing," Lila countered. She reached for Steven's shoulders, hoping to distract him from his current line of questioning.

But Steven caught her hands and held them fast. "Lila, if you don't tell me anything, how can I help you?"

Lila's eyes filled with tears. "Just holding me would be a big help," she said softly.

Steven shook his head. "We have to work this through," he insisted. He raised her hands to his lips and kissed them. "I'm here for you, Lila. But you have to trust me."

Lila sniffed. "I do trust you, Steven," she replied shakily. "But I'm trying so hard to put my life together again, to feel safe. . . ." She looked around the pool house, where she'd been living since the fire. Jessica had tried to convince her to move in with the Wakefields until her parents returned, but Lila wanted to be in her own home—or at least what was left of it. She desperately wanted things to be normal again.

"I promise, you will be safe," Steven said, his voice low and urgent. "As soon as we catch the person who set fire to your house and is trying to frame you for the crime."

Lila nodded reluctantly. "I know. And I can't

tell you how much it means to me to have you here. But I've tried so hard to forget about John . . . about what he did to me. . . ." Her voice broke on a sob.

Steven cupped her chin with his hands. "Tell me about it," he whispered.

Lila looked into Steven's deep brown eyes. She wanted to tell him the whole truth, but she was afraid he would think less of her once he knew. Others had been quick to blame her for what had happened. Lila felt a tear slip down her cheek. *What if Steven says it was all my fault . . . and walks out on me like everyone else?* she worried.

"Don't be afraid, Lila," Steven whispered. "It's going to be OK. I promise."

Lila nodded. She had to trust Steven completely. There was no one else on her side. "I went out with John some time ago," she began, her voice thin and weak.

"Go on," Steven said encouragingly.

Lila swallowed hard and continued. "I was caught totally off guard by him," she admitted. "John had always seemed like such a nice guy. He was quiet, serious, and smart. He's the sports editor for the *Oracle,* and back when . . ." She paused.

"Go on," Steven prompted.

"When John and I started . . . um . . . getting close, he'd just won a special internship in the sports department of the *L.A. Sun*." Lila sniffed. "I was flattered that a guy like that would be interested in me."

"Did you go out with him for very long?" Steven asked gently.

Lila uttered a bitter laugh. "One date," she replied. "We went out for dinner, then took a drive to Miller's Point."

"Is that when he became . . . rough?" Steven asked.

Lila nodded. Memories flooded back to her, the shock and the fear. She felt as if she were in a trance as the story tumbled out. "We were in his car and John wanted to take things further than I was willing to go," she said. "He kissed me so hard, he knocked my head against the door frame. I told him to stop, but he laughed and told me to quit teasing him. When I tried to back away, he grabbed my hair and yanked me toward him."

A fierce look came into Steven's eyes. "Guys like that . . . ," he spat, clenching his fist.

Lila shivered and wrapped her arms around herself. Despite Steven's obvious concern and support, she felt frozen and alone—the same way she'd felt after that horrible night. "I managed to get away from him," she continued. "But my whole world felt totally shattered."

Steven touched the side of her face and smiled gently. "I'm sorry you had to go through that."

Lila's eyes filled with hot tears. "It was so—" She sniffed loudly. "I was so alone. Like now."

"Not now," Steven whispered, taking her into his arms. "You're not alone."

Lila closed her eyes and inhaled deeply, letting Steven's warmth soothe and comfort her.

"What happened after that night?" Steven asked. "It's really important that you tell me everything, Lila."

She nodded and exhaled slowly. "I didn't tell anyone at first because I didn't think anyone would believe me. Also—" Her voice broke on a sob. "I was afraid everyone would say that I got what I deserved, because it was my idea to go to Miller's Point."

Steven shook his head emphatically. "That doesn't make it your fault. He's the jerk for not respecting your limits."

Lila sniffed loudly. His words warmed her heart and gave her strength. "Thank you for saying that, Steven."

"I mean it," he said.

Lila gave him a watery smile. "I know you do. Anyway, after that night, I wanted to forget the whole thing. But then John came to my house a few nights later while I was giving a party, and acted as if nothing had happened."

Steven grimaced as if he'd just tasted something rotten. "What a slime!"

"I know," Lila replied weakly. "Finally, I realized I couldn't keep it a secret anymore. I had to speak out, but I was so afraid. Then another girl came forward and admitted that John had also attacked her. We got together and confronted him publicly, at the Dairi Burger."

"What did he do?" Steven asked.

Lila's heart pounded as she relived those moments when she'd marched right over to John Pfeifer in the crowded Sweet Valley hangout. "He tried to deny everything," she said. "But in the end, everyone at SVH supported us against him."

"Was he formally charged with anything?" Steven inquired.

Lila sighed wearily and shook her head. "No, but everyone knows he tried to rape me. John Pfeifer has been pretty much an outcast ever since."

"That might be a strong motive for revenge," Steven remarked.

Lila immediately jerked upright, her heart leaping to her throat. "Do you think it's possible that John might be out to get me?"

Steven took her into his arms and held her tightly. "I'm going to get to the bottom of this," he promised. "I won't let anyone hurt you again."

Lila's hands trembled as she clasped Steven's strong shoulders. "I'm so afraid," she cried.

Wednesday morning, Devon woke up disoriented. Lying in the strange brass bed, he stared at the yellow ceiling above his head and tried to remember where he was. *A motel?* he wondered.

He pushed himself into a sitting position and rubbed his hand over his eyes. The decor of the room was starkly masculine, and there was a chocolate brown satin comforter on the bed. Bright sunlight streamed in through the casement windows along the east wall. Devon yawned deeply and stretched his arms over his head. As he became alert, he remembered where he was and the events of the previous evening that had brought him there. *I found my uncle Pete,* he thought happily.

Devon tried to rein in his hopes. Nothing had been permanently settled yet, of course. But Devon longed for the time when it might become routine to wake up in this bed, in this room, and get ready for school. . . .

As soon as he was convinced of his uncle's sincerity, Devon would start the process of naming Pete as his legal guardian—and collect the first ten million his father had left him.

Devon pushed back the satin comforter and got

out of bed. After a quick shower in the adjoining bathroom, he got dressed and followed the scent of fresh coffee to the kitchen. Like the rest of the apartment, it was sleek and modern, done in shades of black and beige.

He was surprised to find his uncle already sitting at the table, hunched over a newspaper. Devon's new room was right across from Pete's study. Devon had overheard him in there making phone calls long into the night.

Pete looked up from his newspaper. "Glad to see you're an early riser," he said. "I was afraid you'd be one of those spoiled rich boys that have to be dragged out of bed every morning."

"On the weekends, sometimes," Devon admitted. He helped himself to a cup of coffee and sat down across from his uncle. "I guess I should check out the local high school," he said with some hesitation. Enrolling in a new school was a major commitment; it meant that he intended to stay on permanently. *Is that what my uncle wants too?* Devon wondered.

Pete looked at him incredulously. "Why?"

Devon lifted the coffee cup to his lips and studied his uncle over the rim. "You don't think I should count on being here too long?" he asked directly, dreading the answer.

"I don't think you need it," Pete clarified, surprising

him. "You seem smart enough to me already. Believe me, you'll learn a lot more by sticking with me, kid. Real life is the best classroom in the world. Las Vegas is a laboratory for the study of higher mathematics and human psychology."

Devon took a sip of coffee and set the cup down. He'd never seriously considered dropping out of school. His parents would've had a fit. *But maybe Uncle Pete is right,* Devon reasoned. The more he thought about it, the more the idea appealed to him. "I suppose I could take the high-school equivalency exam when I turn eighteen and go straight to college when I'm ready," he said.

"Sure, whatever," Pete said breezily. "The sky is the limit and you're in the pilot's seat. I won't ask a thing from you, because I can see you've got a good head on your shoulders. You'll be fine no matter what you do."

Devon smiled. "Thanks for the vote of confidence."

Pete pushed aside his newspaper and reached for his coffee cup. "You have total freedom here— no curfews or third degree about where you're going or with whom." His lips twisted into a crooked smile. "Believe me, I know what it's like to live with people who try to control your every move."

Devon nodded. "My parents flipped back and forth between trying to control me and ignoring me. I'm not sure which was worse," he admitted.

Pete gave him an understanding look. "Sounds like the typical Whitelaw upbringing. But you survived it, which is something to be proud of, kid."

Deeply touched, Devon swallowed against the lump in his throat. *Someone actually understands how it was for me,* he thought. *This is what family is all about.*

Devon finished the rest of his coffee and carried the cup to the sink. He turned on the water and began washing the cup, hoping to demonstrate that he didn't consider himself a guest.

"Hey, what do you think you're doing?" his uncle protested.

Devon turned to him and shrugged. "Just thought I'd clean up after myself."

Pete shook his head, frowning. "I pay a very efficient lady to do that sort of thing. You trying to put her out of a job?"

Devon turned off the faucet and dried his hands, leaving the dirty cup in the sink. Obviously it was going to take a while to get the hang of things in his new home, and to figure out what his uncle expected of him. "Are you sure you don't want me to do my fair share, or help out with a few expenses?" he asked.

His uncle chuckled. "You're OK, kid. I appreciate the thought, but I don't want your money. And I especially don't want you making my cleaning lady nervous about her job. I like having you around, that's enough."

Devon felt a warm glow in response. "Maybe I can repay you by fixing you up with Linda," he suggested, half jokingly.

Pete raised his eyebrows. "I wish you could, but I'm afraid it's hopeless."

"It's only hopeless if you don't try," Devon countered, wondering where *that* sentiment came from. He'd always considered himself to be cynical and cool. *When did I turn into such an optimist?* he thought.

Pete shook his head. "I *have* tried," he insisted. "I'll show you." He got up and left the room.

Devon watched him go, puzzling over the situation. His uncle seemed more like a high-school kid than a sophisticated Vegas gambler. *Amazing what a woman can do to a guy,* he thought wryly.

Pete returned to the kitchen with a small package wrapped in silver paper. "I bought this for her last week, but I can't get up the courage to give it to her. She'd probably throw it in my face anyway."

"Why don't you mail it to her?" Devon asked.

Pete curled his fingers around the gift. "She'd probably chuck it into the nearest trash can without opening it," he muttered. "But I have an idea. Why don't you hold on to this, and if you see her later . . ." He shrugged and shot Devon a hopeful look.

Devon frowned. "Where would I see her?"

"You never know." Pete placed the package in Devon's hands and winked. "Vegas is full of surprises, kid."

Devon closed his fist around the gift and made himself a promise. *If helping Pete win back Linda is the only way I can return his hospitality, then that's exactly what I'm going to do!* Devon vowed.

Chapter 4

Surrounded by bright lights, glitzy people, and gambling fervor, Devon held his breath as a pair of dice tumbled across the green baize of the craps table. The shooter was an elderly man dressed in a pale blue polyester leisure suit that was probably from the late 1970s. Devon had a twenty-dollar bet riding on the outcome of the man's turn.

It was early afternoon, but it made no difference. People were decked out in evening wear, most with an alcoholic drink in their hand. No matter the time of day, indoors in a Las Vegas casino seemed to be a consistent experience. Devon himself was wearing a dark blue, three-piece Armani suit borrowed from his uncle. Pete had insisted that projecting a suave, glitzy image was absolutely necessary. "The women will fall at your feet, and the casino pit bosses will favor you with comp dinners and show tickets," he'd told Devon.

The tension around the craps table mounted. Devon watched intently as the dice landed. Nine dots were showing, creating the established point. The shooter would keep rolling the dice until he either matched the nine—in which case he'd win—or until he rolled a seven and lost. Devon felt his blood pumping harder as the suspense was drawn out. Finally, after three more shots, the man rolled a nine.

"All right!" Devon shouted, raising his fist. Several others around the table who'd bet on the man's win joined the cheer. The atmosphere was tacky and artificial, but incredibly thrilling. Devon was having the time of his life. *Thanks, Uncle Pete*, he thought, suppressing a grin.

That morning, Pete had taken him downtown to a respectable-looking photo studio to get a fake ID. Devon had also stopped at a bookstore and picked up a guidebook on Las Vegas and an instruction manual on various casino games. He didn't want to appear ignorant.

His uncle had disappeared hours ago for a private, high-stakes game, so Devon was on his own. He'd made the rounds of the roulette wheels first, and had tucked away a sizable profit—which he'd lost at the blackjack tables. Now, playing craps, it seemed to Devon that his luck was back on the rise. He could easily see how a person might become addicted to gambling.

Standing at the head of the table, the stick man cleared the surface and prepared for another round. Devon's turn was next. A woman with huge red lips, wearing a strapless silver dress, sidled up to him. "My money's on you," she cooed. "Would you like me to kiss the dice for luck?" She walked her fingers up his arm and winked.

Devon felt his face grow warm. This lady wasn't like the immature schoolgirls who'd flirted with him back in Connecticut. She was way out of his league. *But I'm in fantasyland,* he reminded himself. *Anything goes.*

He curved his arm around the woman's bare shoulders. "That would be a total waste, because the dice wouldn't appreciate it," Devon said in a cavalier tone. "But I would." With that, he pressed his lips to hers. Everyone at the table laughed cheerfully.

Devon shook the dice, his blood pumping urgently through his veins. His come-out roll, the first of his turn, was an eleven—an instant win. "Yes!" he cried, applause erupting around him.

Suddenly, Devon caught a glimpse of a tall, slim brunette playing a slot machine. She looked like

Linda Clark, but Devon couldn't tell for sure. When she pulled down the lever of the machine, she shifted sideways, giving Devon a full view of her face. It was Linda.

Devon studied her for a moment. She had the elegant beauty of a fashion model, with smooth, clear skin, high cheekbones, thin eyebrows, and a sharp chin. Her outfit—a short black leather skirt and belted jacket—showed off her curvy shape and fantastic legs.

Devon also noted the cool expression in her eyes and the firm set of her jaw. She hardly seemed to be the open, friendly type. *What if she tells me to get lost?* he wondered, surprised by how intimidated he felt.

He fingered the small wrapped package in his suit jacket pocket. Pete needed his help. *Family means looking out for one another,* Devon told himself. He'd never felt that way growing up in Connecticut, nor had he found that sense of family in Ohio. But now Pete was his family. Devon wanted their relationship to be real, based on more than their common name and background.

"Are you in?" Devon's sultry companion at the craps table asked.

Devon shook his head, watching Linda from the corner of his eye.

The woman flashed him a sexy smile and

handed him one of her business cards. "Later, darling," she whispered suggestively.

Devon slipped the card into his breast pocket, giving her a broad wink. He hurried over to the nearest cashier's cage to cash in his chips. He'd won nearly a hundred dollars that afternoon. *Let's see if my luck holds out when I try to get Linda and Pete back together,* he thought hopefully.

A harrowing headache was pounding in Steven's forehead when he arrived home from the D.A.'s office. He'd spent the entire day going over his notes from the night before, checking countless leads. All of the domestic workers Lila had recently fired had alibis for the night of the Fowler Crest fire.

After numerous phone calls, Steven had also learned that Joan Borden and her daughter, Jacqueline, were living in Spain. Apparently Ms. Borden's luck had improved after her humiliating failure with George Fowler. She'd married a man from Texas with a vast fortune in oil, whom she'd later divorced for an even wealthier Spanish shipping tycoon.

Steven parked his yellow Volkswagen in the driveway and turned off the engine. But he made no move to get out of the car. *How am I going to clear Lila?* he wondered, racking his brain. The D.A. expected him to figure out her motivation for committing the crime. Steven didn't know how much longer he could stall. That morning, Mr. Garrison had eyed him suspiciously when the Fowler case was being discussed at the department meeting.

I need to come up with a viable theory to take to Garrison, Steven thought. He rubbed his hand over his eyes and stared blankly through the windshield. *No . . . I need to find the person who started that fire, and who is trying to frame Lila—after nearly killing her!* he silently amended.

He thought about the fear in Lila's eyes when she'd told him about John Pfeifer. He'd hurt her once, and was obviously prone to violence.

Steven gripped the steering wheel tightly, his fingers turning white. *If that jerk is behind all this . . .* He'd promised Lila he would get to the bottom of things and make her safe again. It was a promise he intended to keep.

Feeling a new sense of determination, Steven grabbed his briefcase and hopped out of the car. He needed to find out as much as he could about John Pfeifer. And he knew just where to start.

Steven found Elizabeth in the backyard, sitting by the pool. He pulled a chair over and sat down facing her. "John Pfeifer," he said without preamble.

Elizabeth blinked. "Whatever happened to 'Hello, how are you?'"

Steven grinned sheepishly. "Hello, how are you?"

"Fine, thanks," Elizabeth muttered dryly. "Now what's this about John Pfeifer?"

Steven took his yellow legal pad and pencil out of his briefcase. "Lila told me about the trouble he caused her a while back," he said.

Elizabeth nodded. "It was really a shock to everyone at SVH. John had always seemed like such a quiet, serious guy—hardly the type you'd expect to get rough with a girl. I think a lot of people believed that Lila was lying. Then Susan Wyler came forward and announced that John had attacked her on a date too."

"But neither girl pressed criminal charges," Steven interjected, shaking his head. If John Pfeifer had had a criminal record, Steven might have been able to talk the D.A. into considering John a likely suspect.

"They didn't have any solid proof," Elizabeth pointed out.

"So he got away with assault and attempted rape," Steven said bitterly. "Twice."

Elizabeth sighed. "I was there when Lila and Susan confronted John about what he'd done to them. It was in the Dairi Burger, in front of lots of witnesses. John denied everything, but no one took his side. He's been pretty much an outcast since then."

Steven scribbled the word *outcast* next to John Pfeifer's name. "What do you think of the guy, personally?" he asked Elizabeth.

Elizabeth tipped her head as she thought. "I once considered him a good friend," she said. "It seems strange now, but when he and Lila first started seeing each other, I was concerned that *she* would end up hurting *him*."

"How do you feel about him now?" Steven asked.

Elizabeth gave him a pointed look. "Now, I wouldn't like to be alone with him in a dark alley," she replied. "In fact, I make it a point not to be alone with him in the *Oracle* office. Which is hard, since he spends so much time in there."

"Doing what?" Steven wanted to know.

Elizabeth shrugged. "Writing and editing sports articles, looking up information on the computer . . . the normal things a sports editor would do. Except in John's case, he spends more time at it than usual since he doesn't have much else going for him."

Steven stiffened. "Looking up information on the computer?" he repeated, bells going off in his head. "You mean like surfing the Net?" The printout on arsonists that someone had mysteriously left on his desk had been downloaded from a Web page.

"All the computers in the *Oracle* office have access to the Internet," Elizabeth confirmed. "John gets a lot of material for his articles from the sports sites on the Web."

Steven tapped the eraser end of the pencil on the arm of the chair. "I think I'll drop by the *Oracle* office and check some things out. When would be a good time?" he asked Elizabeth.

"The office is pretty quiet early in the morning," she replied.

"I want a time when John Pfeifer isn't likely to be there," Steven said.

Elizabeth's eyes narrowed. "John is covering a track meet at Big Mesa after school tomorrow. I can show you around the *Oracle* office then. Although I'm not sure what you're hoping to find," she added.

Steven wrote himself a reminder to clear his schedule for the following afternoon. "Thanks, Liz. That would be helpful."

"But remember, John isn't officially guilty of anything," Elizabeth said.

Steven stiffened. "I'm the one studying prelaw," he retorted. "You don't have to remind me how our legal system works."

Elizabeth raised her chin and shot him a defiant look. "All I meant is that until you have all the facts, you should remain objective and keep an open mind."

Steven bristled. *First my boss and now my sister—why is everyone nagging me about my objectivity?* he thought hotly. "For your information,

Liz, I *am* keeping an open mind. It's my *job* to check out possible leads in this case and try to find the person who set fire to Fowler Crest."

"But you never know when you could be wrong about a person," Elizabeth said. "Think about that, Steven."

Steven glared at her. "If you have something to say, just spit it out."

Elizabeth sighed. "How well do you really know Lila?" she asked.

"I know her very well, thank you," he answered angrily.

"Do you?" Elizabeth challenged. "I'm not saying she's guilty of starting that fire, but if the D.A. is suspicious—"

"The D.A. is wrong!" Steven shouted, cutting her off.

Elizabeth sat up straighter. "Maybe he is. But until you know for sure, don't you think you should use a little more caution?"

"You can't really believe Lila is an arsonist!" Steven said, fuming. "I could imagine Jessica making such a bizarre leap of logic, but I'm surprised to hear all this from you."

Elizabeth shook her head. "No, I don't think Lila is an arsonist. But people can surprise you. I have a feeling that maybe she's not exactly the person you think she is. Especially . . ." She paused. "Steven, can't you see how perfect you and Billie were together? And how wrong you and Lila are?"

Steven gripped the side of the chair, his fingers wrapped tightly around the aluminum frame. "I can't believe this!" he exploded. "I'm trying to solve a criminal case, there's an insane pyromaniac loose in Sweet Valley, and you're giving me advice about my love life?"

Elizabeth chewed her lip. "It's just that I'm concerned for you," she said softly.

"Thanks a lot, Liz," Steven responded bitingly. He stood up abruptly, tipping the chair over on its side, and grabbed his briefcase. "I'm so glad you're interested in truth and justice," he said in a sarcastic tone.

"I am!" Elizabeth pleaded.

Steven's lips twisted into a humorless grin. "Yeah, right," he muttered. He stormed back into the house, his body pulsing with angry determination. He was especially furious with Elizabeth for throwing his broken relationship with Billie up in his face. Billie had dumped him. If it weren't for Lila, he'd still be feeling totally crushed. Now he wanted to show everyone how wrong they were to suspect a girl as sweet and vivacious as Lila of setting fire to her own home.

I have to solve this case, Steven thought, pushing

open the sliding glass patio door. *I have to do it for Lila. And for the sake of my job.* And most of all, Steven wanted to kill any teeny-tiny shadow of doubt he might harbor in his own mind that Lila could actually be guilty.

Devon followed Linda through the casino. In the front lobby, she paused to speak to a woman who was on her way inside. Devon stayed back and watched her through the glass doors, waiting to catch a moment alone with her. But a crowd of senior citizens came in, blocking Devon's view. When they'd cleared the lobby, Linda was gone.

Cursing under his breath, Devon hurried out of the building. The midday desert sun stabbed his eyes, temporarily blinding him. When he could see again, he gazed up and down the street. *Don't tell me I lost her,* he thought, kicking himself.

Suddenly he spotted her walking north on the other side of the street. Devon smiled slowly. He felt as if he were playing the lead in an old-fashioned spy thriller.

Trailing Linda's movements from the corner of his eye, Devon began crossing the busy boulevard. Car horns blared at him as he darted through the heavy traffic, and a gray limousine nearly hit him head-on. By the time Devon made it to the other side of the street, his heart was pounding like a drum from his close brush with disaster. *If this really were a spy movie, I would've insisted on a stunt double for that scene!* he thought wryly.

He saw Linda entering the Brada Hotel on the next block. "Back to work," he muttered as he broke into a run after her. He wasn't about to let her slip out of sight.

Devon finally caught up to her in the lobby of the Brada, just as she was stepping into the elevator. *I've got you now!* he cheered silently. He darted forward and wedged his arm into the narrow gap of the closing elevator doors. A few people glared at him as he pushed his way into the small, crowded space. But Linda's eyes remained focused straight ahead, not even glancing in his direction.

The elevator stopped at several floors on its way up, letting off a few passengers at a time. Finally, only Devon and Linda remained.

Devon cleared his throat, trying to think of an opening line. *"My uncle sent me"?* he mentally rehearsed. *Too lame,* he decided. *"Excuse me, miss, did you know you have a secret admirer"? Way too hokey . . .*

"You're following me, aren't you?" she said abruptly.

Startled, Devon blinked. *Now there's a great opening line,* he thought.

"Don't try to deny it," she warned, her hand

hovering on the elevator alarm switch as she looked him up and down. A silver-and-turquoise bracelet circled her wrist, and her long, tapered fingernails were painted red. "I don't know if I should be flattered or terrified."

Devon raised his hands, palms forward in a pose of surrender. "I didn't mean to scare you, honestly."

"Then why are you stalking me?" she demanded.

"I'm not," Devon assured her, shaking his head vehemently. "My name is Devon Whitelaw. Pete is my uncle."

She glared at him with an astonished look in her eyes. "You have my condolences," she said, then turned her attention to the lighted floor numbers on the overhead panel.

Devon pushed his hand through his hair and let out a frustrated sigh. "Don't you want to know why he sent me?" he asked, hoping to pique her curiosity.

"Not really," she answered blandly.

The elevator stopped at the penthouse floor and the doors opened. She stepped out without a backward glance, her back stiff and her shoulders straight.

"Wait," Devon called, following behind her.

She stopped at the door to one of the suites and inserted a plastic key card into the lock. "Go away," she said over her shoulder. "And tell your uncle to do the same."

"But you don't understand," Devon insisted.

Linda gave him a withering look. "I do understand, all too well," she replied. "Now if you'll excuse me . . ." She slipped into the suite.

"Wait," Devon said again as she was about to close the door on his face. "Pete sent me to tell you he really misses you, and that he still cares about you—a lot."

"Your uncle cares for nobody but himself," she said, her voice edged with bitterness. "That's a warning to you," she added.

"You're wrong," Devon countered. He took out the wrapped box his uncle had given him that morning. "Pete asked me to give you this. He was afraid you wouldn't accept it if he gave it to you in person."

"He's right." Linda leaned against the open door and eyed the gift as if it were a poisonous snake. "And why should I accept it from you?"

"Because I went to a lot of trouble to get it to you." Devon flashed her his best charming smile. "I was nearly run down by traffic when I crossed the street to get here," he added.

"Am I supposed to be impressed?" she muttered. But she did take the box, to Devon's great relief. He would have hated having to return it to his uncle in defeat.

Linda tore off the silver paper, revealing a blue velvet jewelry case. She lifted the lid and rolled her eyes. "Something shiny and expensive," she muttered caustically, snapping the case closed.

Devon had gotten a brief glimpse of the diamond-studded gold watch inside. *"Shiny and expensive" sums it up quite well,* he thought.

Linda slipped the case into the pocket of her tailored leather jacket. "Does Pete think this little trinket will fix everything between us?"

"It's a start, isn't it?" Devon replied. "All he's asking for is a second chance."

"Pete's already had dozens of second chances," Linda said, shaking her head. "When you see your uncle, tell him money can't buy love."

Don't I know it, Devon silently agreed, his heart sinking. He'd grown up in a home where money had been a tool to gain power and control. Love and money didn't seem to mix well together.

But Devon had a feeling that his uncle really did love Linda, even if he did have a crass way of showing it. "I can understand you're mad at Pete," he said. "But won't you at least consider talking to him?"

"OK," Linda replied.

Devon blinked. "You will?" he asked hopefully.

Linda raised her eyebrows. "I'll *consider* it,"

she clarified. "See you around." With that, she shut the door on Devon.

Devon sighed and shook his head. "Women!" he muttered under his breath. But he felt good about what he'd just done for his uncle. Pete didn't want his money, and he trusted Devon with matters of the heart.

If things go right with Linda, I'll have a new aunt soon . . . and maybe a few baby cousins running around the apartment, Devon thought. He was surprised at how much the idea appealed to him.

Chapter 5

After his encounter with Linda, Devon spent a few hours downstairs in the Brada Hotel casino. His good luck stayed with him. By the time he had to leave to meet his uncle, Devon had nearly doubled his money. *I could get used to this real easy*, he thought as he waited in line at the cashier's cage to cash in his playing chips.

When Devon arrived at the Starscape, Uncle Pete was already in the bar, waiting for him. Seated in one of the high-back leather chairs, Pete lifted his glass in a welcoming gesture. "How was your first day on the loose in Las Vegas?" he asked.

Devon sat in the chair across from him. "I saw Linda," he blurted excitedly.

Pete froze, his glass halfway to his mouth. "And?"

"I gave her your present," Devon supplied. "She opened it."

Pete took a long drink and set the glass back down on the table. "Did she like it?" he asked.

"She was . . ." Devon paused, choosing his words carefully. His uncle was watching him with his eyes wide open, like a puppy expecting a treat. "I think she was very surprised," Devon said finally.

Pete nodded thoughtfully. "How did she look? What was she wearing?"

Devon recalled the details for his uncle. "She had on a black leather skirt and jacket. It wasn't like my jacket, though. It was more like a lady's suit blazer, but made out of leather. She wore it with a silver belt."

"Yeah, I know which one you mean," Pete said. "It looks great on her, doesn't it?"

"She's very . . . pretty," Devon remarked.

"Was she wearing a sapphire bracelet?" Pete asked. "I gave it to her for her birthday," he added.

Devon shook his head. "I did notice a bracelet, but it was silver and turquoise."

Pete chuckled. "She still has that? I bought it for pocket change the day she dragged me to a hokey craft fair in Arizona," he said with a wistful smile. "That was more than a year ago!"

Devon grinned. "Obviously she still cares about you," he said.

Pete blinked. "She said that?"

Devon glanced off to the side. *Poor guy's got it bad*, he thought. He didn't want to come out and tell his uncle what Linda *had* said.

Devon took a deep breath and let it out slowly. "Not exactly," he replied, hedging. "I think she's mad, but not so much that there's no hope for the two of you. I did get the impression that your gift insulted her, though."

Pete reeled back. "You're kidding! That watch was top-class, genuine all the way. It cost me a bundle."

"That's just it," Devon began cautiously. "She seemed to think you were trying to buy her."

"Buy her?" Pete said, clearly astonished. "That's ridiculous! I really care about Linda."

"Maybe it's time to try a different approach," Devon suggested.

His uncle laughed. "What do you have in mind, kid?"

Devon imagined what he would do if he ever found a girl he could love, one who would love him in return—for *himself,* not his money. She would have to be intelligent, kind, someone he could relax with . . .

Devon leaned back, bracing his elbows on the

arms of the chair. *What if I did find this dream girl . . . and then lost her?* he wondered. *What if we got into a big fight and she refused to see me, like Linda and Pete?* Just thinking about it made Devon ache, as if a sharp knife were stabbing his heart. "I'd never give up on her," he swore passionately. "No matter what it takes. I'd have to win her back—or die trying!"

Pete stared blankly, then clapped his hands a few times. "That was great, kid!" he said, gently mocking him. "Such heart-wrenching emotion and conviction! You could take that act all the way to Hollywood."

Devon rolled his eyes, frustrated with his uncle's stubbornness. "I mean it," he insisted. "If I loved a girl, believe me, she'd *know* it!"

Pete loosened his blue silk tie and crossed his arms. "So tell me. What would you do if you were in my position?" he challenged.

Devon considered the question carefully. "I'd make her understand how I feel about her," he replied. "I'd write her a poem . . . send her flowers, balloons, funny cards, singing telegrams—"

"And you'd turn into a sap," Pete interjected with a twisted grin.

Devon shrugged. "I said no matter what it takes."

Pete snorted. "That's wimp stuff."

"But it works!" Devon argued. "I'll even write the poem, order the flowers . . . whatever."

Pete curved his hands around the base of his glass and lowered his eyes. "I don't know. All that flowers-and-candy garbage . . . ," he began, his voice trailing off. "It's just not my style."

Devon gave his uncle a sharp look. "So change your style," he responded matter-of-factly. "Don't you think Linda is worth the effort?"

"Of course she is," Pete answered. He rubbed his hand over his chin and exhaled a deep breath. "OK, flowers . . . and a little sparkly something to go with them. Sentimental garbage with the dazzle of a high-carat trinket on the side. What woman can resist that combination?"

Devon threw up his hands. "And I thought *I* was stubborn," he muttered.

Pete lifted his glass. "It's just a matter of spreading out your bets, kid," he said, saluting him with his drink. "And with your help, how can I lose?"

Devon squirmed in his seat. Being in charge of getting his uncle's love life back on track was an awesome responsibility. "I'll do my best," he said. "I can't make any promises, though."

Pete's expression grew serious. "Of course you can't," he agreed. "But before you came along, I'd lost all hope of ever winning Linda back. You've made me see that I might have another chance."

Deeply moved, Devon swallowed against the thickening lump in his throat. "Anytime," he quipped, feeling suddenly shy.

Pete gulped down the contents of his glass. "Come on, let's get out of here," he said, rising to his feet. "I'm in the mood for a classy dinner tonight."

They took a taxi to a restaurant a few miles away from the Strip that specialized in North African cuisine. Devon offered to pay the driver out of his day's winnings, but Pete refused to accept even that. "You hold on to your cash, kid," he told Devon. "No winning streak lasts forever."

Devon thought about that as he followed his uncle into the restaurant. Pete hadn't inherited any of the Whitelaw fortune, and he didn't have a job. Devon wondered how he could afford to live in a swanky apartment, buy custom-tailored suits, *and* shower Linda with lavish presents. It seemed Pete's only income was the money he earned from gambling. "I take it you've had a few ups and downs over the years?" Devon asked.

Pete smirked. "You could say that."

The walls of the foyer were draped in red velvet trimmed with gold tassels. A curtain of twisted steel strands hung across the arched inner doorway. They made a soft, metallic sound like jingling keys when anyone swept them aside to walk through. The strains of Arabic music filled the air, along with the fragrance of exotic herbs and spices. Devon might have believed he were in Morocco or Tangier, if it weren't for the slot machines on the side wall. They seemed to yell out loud and clear, *"You're in Las Vegas, buddy!"*

A group of people were lined up at the maitre d' stand, waiting to be seated. A harried-looking young woman was marking off names on her clipboard—presumably her list of that evening's dinner reservations—and answering the wall phone beside her, which rang constantly.

"Looks busy tonight," Devon remarked to his uncle.

Pete shrugged. "I hope that means the food is good."

"You didn't happen to call for reservations, did you?" Devon asked.

"This was strictly spur of the moment," Pete said. "After all, how was I supposed to know we'd have cause to celebrate this evening?"

Devon looked around, shaking his head. Several people were squeezed together on a velveteen divan, a few more leaning against the wall. Everyone looked hungry and bleak, as if they'd been waiting a long time. "I think we picked a bad night to pop in without calling ahead," he muttered.

Pete smiled. "No problem."

"No solution," Devon shot back.

Pete chuckled, shaking his head. "You may be smart, but you're not very creative."

"How's this for a creative solution—let's order a pizza and have it delivered while we wait for a table," Devon suggested jokingly.

"We'll be seated within ten minutes," Pete said.

"Not likely," Devon muttered.

"Care to make a small wager on it?" Pete challenged. "Twenty bucks says we'll have the best table in the house within ten minutes."

Devon laughed. "You're on, Uncle. But let's make it thirty bucks."

Pete raised one eyebrow, his lips twitching at the corners. "OK, Mr. High Roller. Thirty it is." They shook hands on the bet.

"Now watch closely, kid." Pete winked. "You may learn something. First we have to wait for the right moment. . . ."

Just then, a man wearing a dark suit came out of the dining room and went over to talk to the woman at the reservations stand.

"There's the maitre d'," Pete whispered, checking his watch. "Time check: nine minutes, fifteen seconds left to go. Kiss your thirty dollars goodbye, kid."

Devon folded his arms. "We'll see about that,"

he mumbled under his breath as he followed his uncle to the head of the line.

"Dana, how are you?" Pete said, giving the reservations lady a bright, expansive smile. "It's been a while, hasn't it? I almost didn't recognize you. You got your hair cut, didn't you?"

The woman's eyes narrowed slightly, obviously caught off guard. "Why, yes," she replied, covering her surprise with a smile. "It's a bit more blond too."

Pete nodded appreciatively. "It looks stunning." Then he turned to the maitre d'. "Pete Whitelaw," he said, introducing himself as he shook the man's hand. "Is Ibrahim around this evening?"

Who's Ibrahim? Devon wondered as he looked on from the sidelines. He couldn't figure out what was going on.

"I'm sorry, Mr. Filali is not on the premises," the maitre d' told Pete.

Pete appeared crestfallen. "That's too bad. Ibrahim and I have been talking about getting together for years. . . ." He went on with a long, made-up story about how he would be flying out of Las Vegas in a few hours. "I didn't make a reservation this evening because I wanted to surprise Ibrahim."

Devon covered his mouth to keep himself from laughing.

The maitre d' apologized on behalf of absent Ibrahim, whoever he was, and invited Pete to stay for dinner. Less than a minute later, Devon and his uncle were led to the restaurant's VIP Garden Room.

Surrounded by tropical plants, Devon and Pete sat on cushions at a low, ornately decorated table. "OK, you win," Devon said grudgingly, counting out thirty dollars. He pushed the bills across the table.

"I did, didn't I?" Pete said, beaming. He slipped the cash into his inside jacket pocket. "I love winning!"

"I see you've gotten over your aversion to accepting my money," Devon remarked dryly.

Pete raised his eyebrows. "This is *my* money, kid. That's what winning means."

Devon chuckled. "I don't mind, really. It was worth the entertainment of watching you in action. But you might have told me you were friends with some of the people who work here," he complained.

Pete shook his head. "I don't know anyone who works here."

Devon frowned. "But what about that woman, Dana, and that Ibrahim guy you asked to see?"

Pete nodded. "Ibrahim Filali is the owner. I've never met him, but his name is printed in gold letters right on the front door. And as for Dana, I heard her say her name when she answsered the phone."

"But you knew that she'd recently gotten her hair cut," Devon pointed out.

Pete grinned. "That's where a sharp eye comes in handy," he said. "Didn't you notice how she kept fidgeting with the ends of her hair, as if she were trying to get used to the short length?"

Devon stared at him incredulously. "That's amazing. But weren't you worried that she'd call your bluff and tell you to get lost?"

"That's always a possibility," Pete admitted laughingly. "But think about it. This is a tourist town. These people see hundreds of new faces each week. They can't remember everyone, nor do they want to risk their jobs by offending someone who might turn out to be an important customer. It's safer for them to play along."

A waiter dressed in a flowing caftan, with cloth slippers and a fez, brought them menus and filled their water goblets. He recited the evening's specials and took their drink orders.

"But what if Ibrahim Filali had been here tonight?" Devon asked after the waiter left.

Pete shrugged. "I would've done the same thing." He leaned forward, dropping his voice. "The owner of this restaurant is in business to make money. Happy customers are even more important to him than they are to the help. What makes you think he'd turn us away?"

"Right," Devon muttered, opening his menu. He wasn't sure if he was as impressed by his uncle's sly manipulations as Pete himself seemed to be. *But who am I to judge him?* Devon asked himself. Obviously Pete had learned to survive after being thrown out of the Whitelaw family. And Devon wasn't the most honest and open person on earth either. He hadn't told his uncle the truth regarding his inheritance and the conditions of his father's will.

Maybe I should drop the pretense and be totally honest with Pete, Devon thought. He hated having a lie between them.

Devon set the menu aside and cleared his throat. "There's something we need to talk about . . . ," he began.

"Yeah, I know," Pete interjected. "Are we hungry enough for the seven-course chef's special, or do we go à la carte?"

Devon drummed his fingers nervously on his knees. Maybe this wasn't the best time to admit his lie to his uncle. There was a chance Pete wouldn't take it well, and Devon hated the idea of ruining things between them so soon. The truth would have to wait.

Devon grinned, masking his worries. "I vote for the seven courses," he told his uncle. "I am a growing boy, you know."

Pete feigned a fierce, insulted look. "And I'm not? Are you trying to tell me I'm over the hill, kid?"

Devon shrugged. "You might have a few good years left," he teased, trying not to smile.

"John normally uses this computer," Elizabeth explained to her brother as she showed him around the *Oracle* office after school.

She and Steven hadn't exchanged more than a few sentences since their argument the previous day. Elizabeth wanted to clear the air between them, but she didn't know what to say. She hadn't changed her mind about his relationship with Lila. But she felt obligated to help him anyway, because he was her brother.

"Who else uses this computer?" Steven asked as his gaze swept the immediate area.

Elizabeth shrugged. "Anyone. There aren't enough computers for everyone to have their own," she explained. "But we all tend to stick with a particular unit."

Steven nodded thoughtfully. "And this is where John Pfeifer tends to stick?"

Elizabeth pressed her bottom lip between her teeth to keep from blurting out an objection. She wasn't entirely comfortable with Steven's suspicions about John. There was no proof that he had been anywhere near Fowler Crest the night of the fire. Steven seemed to be on a desperate crusade to prove Lila's innocence and was grasping at any outside chance to pin the guilt on someone other than his new girlfriend. Elizabeth was afraid Steven would end up hurt in the end.

"This is John's desk," she said tersely as she walked over to a workstation near the window. Several notes, books, pencils, and personal articles were scattered across the surface. A half-eaten candy bar was rolled up in its wrapper, and an open can of ProSport lemon drink was perched on a pile of wire-bound notebooks.

Steven began riffling through John's things. Watching him, Elizabeth's uneasiness grew. "Isn't this a violation of privacy?" she protested.

Steven acted as if he hadn't heard her remark. He picked up a sheet of paper from John's desk. "This is very familiar," he murmured as he examined it closely.

Curious, Elizabeth glanced at it. "It's just a rough draft of an article John's working on," she said.

Steven looked up, his brown eyes alight with excitement. "But the words are printed at a slant, and the margins are uneven." He eagerly reached for John's other papers, knocking over a thick dictionary and nearly upsetting the can of ProSport.

Elizabeth grabbed the can just in time. "You could at least be a little more careful," she uttered reproachfully. "It's bad enough you're invading the guy's privacy. Do you have to trash his desk too?"

Steven looked at her with a blank expression. "What do you mean?"

Elizabeth scowled at him. "This," she said, setting the can back down on the desk. "John is innocent until proven guilty, remember. He doesn't deserve to have ProSport spilled all over his things."

Steven glanced at the bright yellow can and wrinkled his nose. "That stuff is nasty," he spat. "John Pfeifer must be a weirdo if he drinks it."

Elizabeth sniffed indignantly. "Todd drinks it."

"I rest my case," Steven uttered dryly.

"What's that supposed to mean?" Elizabeth asked, her eyes shooting daggers at her brother.

"Any guy who would put up with you . . . ," Steven replied, shaking his head.

Elizabeth folded her arms and glared at him.

Steven chuckled. "Lighten up, Liz. I was just kidding."

"Oh," Elizabeth muttered. Relaxing slightly, she cracked a smile.

"Tell me about these printouts," Steven said,

handing her one of the papers. "Every one is printed slightly off center."

Elizabeth glanced at the copy and frowned, still not sure what he was getting at. "The sheet feeder on one of the printers doesn't work right," she explained. "We're waiting to have it fixed. But why do you think it's such a big deal?"

"I'm not a hundred percent sure yet," he said. "But I think I'm finally on the right trail."

Elizabeth rolled her eyes. "Whatever you say," she replied. Just then, she caught a glimpse of someone at the door. She turned to see who it was, and her heart stopped. She gasped, clutching Steven's shoulder.

John Pfeifer stood there, glaring at her, his fists clenched at his sides.

Chapter 6

Steven shrugged Elizabeth's hand off his shoulder as he mentally compared the papers on John's desk with the printout on arsonists he'd received anonymously. The slightly skewed printing was identical. He was almost sure. *The Web page must have come through the same printer,* he thought excitedly.

He felt Elizabeth give his shoulder a hard shake. "What is it?" he grumbled, scowling at her. Elizabeth's face was as white as chalk as she stared at something behind him. He jerked his head around and saw a guy skulking across the office toward them.

"What do you think you're doing, going through my stuff?" the guy demanded.

Steven slowly straightened and replaced the

papers on John's desk. A feeling of hot, raw anger surged through him. "You must be John Pfeifer," he said, forcing his voice to maintain a level tone. He kept his hands at his sides, even though he was itching to wrap them around the creep's meaty throat. Steven hated him for what he'd done to Lila . . . and for what he might have done.

"What's going on?" John asked.

"I can explain," Elizabeth blurted, her face turning bright pink now.

"So can I," Steven said, taking charge. He leaned back against the side of the desk and folded his arms. "I'm Steven Wakefield."

"I know who you are," John snapped. "What I want to know is what you're doing at my desk."

"I'm with the D.A.'s office," Steven continued, "looking into the Fowler Crest fire. We're pretty sure it was arson."

"What does that have to do with me?" John questioned.

Elizabeth cleared her throat. "Nothing, most likely. But Steven thought . . . you see, he . . . um . . ."

Steven shot her a silencing look and turned to John. "Have you been following the story at all?" he asked in a deceptively casual tone.

John snorted. "I read the newspaper and watch the news, just like everyone else. But that doesn't explain why you're going through my things."

"Doesn't it?" Steven challenged.

"You don't scare me," John said. "Because I don't have anything to hide. But unless you have a search warrant, get away from my stuff."

Steven pushed himself off the desk immediately. "No problem," he said with a wide-eyed look of forced innocence.

Elizabeth's hand trembled as she brushed her fingers over her lips. Steven could see how uncomfortable she was about the confrontation, but he pressed on. He had a job to do.

"By the way, John, where were you the night the fire broke out at Fowler Crest?" Steven asked.

"I don't have to answer any of your questions," John retorted. "But just for the record, I was out bowling with some friends—until very late."

Steven sniffed. "I didn't know you had any friends."

Elizabeth made a small, gasping sound and turned away, shaking her head.

John Pfeifer uttered a derisive laugh. "I still have a few," he spat. "Lila Fowler hasn't managed to turn *everyone* against me—although she certainly tried."

Steven nodded. "I take it you're very angry with her for ruining your life."

"If you're making accusations, you'd better have some solid proof," John warned. "And it better be

111

more than the word of a bored, spoiled rich girl."

Steven clenched his fists, digging his thumbnails into his palms as he fought to keep his fury under control. "Seems to me you didn't always feel that way about Lila," he muttered tightly. "I heard you two even went out on a date . . . *once*."

A wounded look flared in John's eyes, reminding Steven of a beaten puppy. "Lila Fowler is the type of girl who destroys anyone who cares about her," John said, his voice raw with emotion. "If you know what's good for you, Wakefield, you'll stay as far away from Lila as possible."

On his way to see Linda that afternoon, Devon stopped at the flower shop in the lobby of her hotel. *Is she the roses type or mixed bouquet?* he wondered as he studied the array of cut flowers in the florist's case. *Definitely roses,* he finally decided. *Red roses.*

Devon bought a dozen long-stemmed red roses. He considered adding a frilly, gushy card, but decided against it. He and his uncle had worked out a compromise: the flowers *and* the expensive bauble in Devon's pocket. Pete hadn't yet agreed to any of Devon's other sentimental suggestions, but the flowers were a good start.

Feeling optimistic about his mission, Devon rode the elevator to Linda's suite. He glanced at the white florist's box in his arms and chuckled. "I'll have my uncle writing poetry to the woman before this is over," he muttered under his breath.

Devon felt a moment's insecurity when he knocked on Linda's door. *What if she throws the flowers in my face and warns me to stay away from her?* he worried. *What if she calls security and has me thrown out? What if she calls the police and tells them I'm stalking her? What if . . .*

Suddenly the door opened wide. "Devon?" Linda gasped incredulously. "What are you doing—"

"Can I come in?" Devon asked, flashing her his most charming smile.

Linda sighed. "I told you yesterday that—"

Devon cut her off again. "These are from my uncle," he said, holding the long flower box out to her.

Linda glanced at the offering. "What am I going to do with that man?" she said in a weary-sounding voice. But she stood aside and waved Devon into her suite.

Devon stifled a triumphant cheer as he entered. Linda shut the door and led him into the sitting room. "Make yourself comfortable," she told him.

Devon glanced around the room. Everything was pink—the curtains, the carpet, the sofa and cushioned chairs, the clock on the wall. Even the framed prints depicted pink irises. The only thing that wasn't pink was the glass-and-chrome coffee table. It was the ugliest hotel suite he'd ever seen.

Devon sat down on one of the pink chairs. "Interesting decor," he remarked, trying to be polite.

Linda snorted. "Sort of like being trapped in a vat of strawberry mousse," she muttered dryly.

She and Devon laughed. "Why are you here, really?" she asked him.

"Because Pete asked me to come," he told her honestly. "He totally blames himself for ruining things between you two."

"He should," she retorted. "He *did* ruin everything."

"And he's been kicking himself ever since," Devon said. "But he really wants another chance." He leaned forward and set the flower box on the coffee table.

Linda opened the box cautiously, as though she expected the contents to jump out at her. She carefully peeled back the green tissue paper wrapping inside. "They're beautiful," she whispered, lifting one rose from the box. She held the red blossom to her nose and inhaled. "They smell nice too."

Devon beamed. "Pete is really a considerate guy, don't you think?"

Linda snickered. "I'd better go put these in water."

Devon watched her go. *I told you flowers would do the trick, Uncle Pete,* he thought, grinning from ear to ear. And red roses had been an inspired choice.

Linda returned a moment later with the flowers in a glass vase and set the arrangement down on the coffee table. "I love them," she said. Then she gave Devon a narrow-eyed glare. "But don't you tell your good-for-nothing uncle I said that!"

Devon smiled. "I dare you to tell him yourself."

"You're Pete's nephew, all right," she said wryly. "I'd recognize that smart-mouth attitude anywhere."

But Devon could see the amused sparkle in her dark eyes. This visit was going even better than he'd hoped. He thought about the small package in the pocket of his jacket and wondered if he should give it to her at all. She hadn't been nearly as impressed with the diamond watch he'd delivered the day before as she was now by the roses. Devon hated to risk the gains he'd just made by offending her again with an expensive trinket.

But this is Pete's romance, Devon reminded himself. It wasn't up to him to call the shots.

Devon inhaled deeply and took the plunge. "My uncle also wanted you to have this," he said as he nervously handed over the small wrapped package.

"For me?" Linda said with a giggle.

Seeing her happy expression as she opened the gift, Devon relaxed.

"Oh, wow!" she breathed as she held up a dazzling diamond necklace. The gems sparkled with countless points of dancing light.

Devon blinked. "It's something, all right!" he uttered, totally astonished. *Pete must have spent a small fortune on that,* he thought.

Linda tucked it back into the case and snapped the lid shut. "Thanks for bringing this to me, Devon. It's beautiful."

"Can I tell my uncle you said that?" he asked.

Linda nodded. "But play down how I said it," she added, winking.

Devon smiled. It seemed they were finally getting somewhere. *Good thing too,* he thought. He wondered how much longer his uncle could afford giving Linda such expensive presents. *Even a crafty high roller must have his limits,* Devon reasoned.

Lila caught herself humming as she set a vase of yellow flowers on the table in the pool house that evening. For the first time since the fire, she felt a little like her old self. Steven was due to arrive any minute, and Lila was eagerly looking forward to seeing him again. She had stopped at various shops on the way home from school and had picked up everything she needed for a romantic dinner for two.

Lila stood back for a final inspection. She'd grown tired of eating off the cheap dishes that were stocked in the pool house kitchen, so she'd splurged on making herself feel at home. She'd purchased a set of fine porcelain china, crystal stemware, and a white linen tablecloth with delicate blue embroidery along the edges.

The flowers, blue linen napkins, and blue tapers in a new silver candelabra added the finishing touches. *I should have picked up some silverware,* she thought as she critically eyed the cheap stainless set on the table. "Oh, well, these will have to do for now," she grumbled.

Lila smiled as she set a book of matches next to the candles. The matches were from Chez Costa, a souvenir of her first date with Steven.

Lila went to the small refrigerator and began taking out the various containers of food she'd purchased at Seasons, a local gourmet shop. "A potato-chip-and-onion-dip type of guy *indeed!*" she muttered under her breath, recalling the words Jessica had used to describe Steven. "That girl doesn't know what she's talking about!" Lila was sure he'd be impressed with all the trouble she'd gone to that evening.

She prepared a bowl of cracked ice, then scooped black caviar into a smaller bowl and nestled it into the ice. Next, she arranged pâté, assorted cheeses, and stuffed mushrooms on a platter. Steven arrived just as she was tossing the mesclun salad greens with olive oil vinaigrette.

"Good evening," she said as he came bounding through the screen door.

Steven barely glanced at the table. Lila felt a twinge of disappointment, but, seeing the excited look on his face, she shrugged it off. "What's up?" she asked anxiously.

Steven grabbed her shoulders and gave her a quick, firm kiss. "I think I hit pay dirt," he said.

Lila's eyes opened wide and her heart lurched. "Did you find out who set the fire?" she asked breathlessly.

Steven nodded. "I'm pretty sure I did."

Lila sank into the closest chair and wrapped her arms around herself. A shiver ran up and down her spine. *I don't want to know,* she realized. Hearing the name of the person who had tried to burn down her house with her in it would make the nightmare seem too real. "I wish it would all go away," she whimpered.

Steven squatted in front of her chair and pulled her into his arms. "It will, Lila," he whispered, caressing her hair. "Soon."

Lila hugged him close, drawing comfort from his warm strength as well as from his reassuring words. "Who is it, Steven?" she asked finally.

Steven rose to his feet and reached for her hand. "Let me show you what I've found," he said, leading her over to the couch. He opened his briefcase and took out some papers. "Look at these."

Lila glanced at the top page and shrugged. "This is the profile of a typical arsonist, but how does that pinpoint who started the fire in my house?" she asked, nonplussed.

Steven directed her attention to the other pages. "Compare that with these."

Lila skimmed the second page, which was part of an interview with Mr. Featherston, Sweet Valley's track coach. "I still don't know what you're getting at," she said impatiently.

"Notice any similarities between the two?" Steven prompted.

Lila felt much too distraught for a guessing game. "Just tell me!" she snapped.

Steven grinned sheepishly. "Last week, that Web page printout was left on my desk anonymously. I asked everyone in the D.A.'s office, but no one there sent it to me, and it didn't come by way of the front desk. That really bothered me. I mean, why would someone download this information and then be so mysterious about it?"

"It does seem strange," Lila agreed.

"Anyway, I noticed how the print is slightly skewed," he said, pointing out the slanting margins on the top and bottom of the page.

Lila drew in a quick breath as she suddenly understood. "It's the same way in the sports article!"

"Which I found this afternoon in the *Oracle* office—on John Pfeifer's desk," Steven told her. "I think this just about proves that he's the one who put the arsonist profile in my box. He must've thought you fit the characteristics, and he wanted me to suspect you."

"And you think he's . . ." Lila gulped. "You think John set fire to my house and tried to frame me?"

"That's exactly what I think!" Steven replied.

Lila blinked, her head reeling. She was utterly speechless. She lowered her gaze to the papers in her hand and stared at the black print until the letters seemed to dance across the page. *John Pfeifer!* she thought, her heart pounding like a kettledrum.

In the span of a few seconds, Lila relived the horror of that fateful night at Miller's Point. In her mind's eye, she saw John's face twisted into a strange, ugly mask. His cruel laughter rang in her ears, scraping her nerves. She relived his hot breath on her face, his hands gripping her, his teeth grinding against her lips. She felt the sharp blow to her head when it had slammed against the door frame of his car.

That memory gave way to Lila's recent horror. She could almost feel the heat of the flames when she'd woken up on the divan in the living room . . . the thick smoke filling her lungs, choking her . . . Lila thought of the day she'd returned to Fowler Crest from the hospital. She'd found everything in ruins and all the mementos of her life destroyed.

Lila felt tears pooling in her eyes as she looked up at Steven. "He really hates me, doesn't he?" she whispered.

Steven draped his arm around her shoulders. "John Pfeifer is obviously off-balance mentally," he said. "Most criminals are. But don't worry, Lila." He kissed the side of her face. "I'm going to have him put away soon, and he'll never hurt you again."

Lila rested her head on Steven's shoulder. "Have I told you how much I appreciate all you've done for me?" she whispered.

Steven brushed his fingers through her hair. "Just doing my job," he quipped. "I'm going to present this evidence to the D.A. tomorrow. It's only a matter of time until John Pfeifer is brought to justice."

Lila sighed. "And everyone will finally know I didn't try to burn down my own house."

"I suggest we make a date for this weekend to celebrate our success," Steven said. "I mean a *real* date . . . with dinner and dancing. And *not* to talk business."

Lila smiled and threw her arms around his neck. "That sounds wonderful," she said, punctuating her words with a kiss. "Speaking of dinner, have I got a surprise for you!"

She scooted off the couch and pulled him up by the hand. "You're going to love this!" she said, sitting him down at the table.

Lila set the caviar and appetizer platter on the table. "This is just the first course," she explained. "We also have vichyssoise, mesclun salad, chilled escargots in a white wine sauce, braised salmon with capers and pecans, and for dessert, hazelnut torte." Beaming proudly, she stood back and watched his reaction.

But Steven didn't seem as enthusiastic as she'd hoped. He shrugged and helped himself to a bit of pâté, a small spoonful of caviar, and a slice of Camembert cheese.

"I hope you like it," Lila said, taking the seat across from him.

"I do," Steven replied, chuckling. "But if I don't, it's not a problem at all. Guido's Pizza Palace delivers, and I know their number by heart."

Lila flinched, stung by his cavalier attitude—

she'd gone to so much trouble. But then she decided he couldn't have been serious, and that he was just teasing her.

Steven's probably trying to cheer me up, she reasoned. After all, he was her hero. Lila trusted he would never do anything to deliberately hurt her feelings. Her life seemed to be getting back on track finally, and it was Steven she had to thank for that. *Maybe I should lighten up and enjoy myself,* Lila thought.

"The roses really impressed Linda," Devon told his uncle that evening. They were having dinner at the Longhorn Grill, which was located across the street from Pete's apartment building.

"She loved them," Devon added.

The corners of Pete's lips twitched slightly, as if he was trying not to smile. He was obviously happy that Linda had been pleased. "How nice for the roses," he quipped.

Seeing right through his uncle's brusque facade, Devon grinned broadly. "I'm telling you, Linda's crazy about you," he insisted.

Pete pointed his knife at Devon's plate. "They're charging me a small fortune for that slab of meat. Eat it before it gets cold."

"She put the roses in water first thing," Devon continued, undaunted. "That's a good sign."

Pete raised one eyebrow and stared at him. "Oh, great. Now you're reading *signs* like a gypsy fortune-teller?" he teased.

"Sure," Devon replied. "A bad sign would be if she dumped them in the trash. Work with me here, Uncle Pete. This isn't brain surgery or rocket science. You'll get the hang of it."

Pete shook his head, laughing. "I used to think you were just like me twenty-five years ago, but I was wrong," he said, his blue eyes twinkling with humor. "I was never such a smart-alecky, know-it-all brat like you!"

Devon bowed his head as if he'd just been applauded. "You stick with me, and Linda will be yours. The roses were just the beginning. We'll melt her heart with all kinds of romantic gestures, and win her back forever."

Pete took a roll from the breadbasket and began buttering it. "Whatever you say, kid. But did you remember to tell her the roses were from me, and not from you?"

"Of course!" Devon responded. "But I told her the necklace was from me," he added jokingly.

Pete narrowed his eyes, feigning a vicious look, and shook his fist threateningly. Devon tipped his head back and laughed.

"Eat your dinner!" Pete growled.

Devon eagerly sawed off a chunk of his thick

T-bone steak and speared it with his fork. "This is really good, by the way," he commented.

"Yeah, well . . . I'm glad you like it," Pete said. He hooked his elbow over the back of the chair and gestured with his hand as he spoke. "What did Linda say about the necklace?"

"She loved it," Devon answered. "Actually, her first words were, 'It's gorgeous.'" He popped the meat into his mouth and chewed slowly.

Pete exhaled a deep, satisfied sigh. "You did good, kid. Congratulations," he said. "The roses were a brilliant touch."

"Thanks," Devon replied, gratified by his uncle's appreciation.

"We deserve to go out and celebrate," Pete suggested.

Devon glanced around the restaurant. "Seems to me we're already out," he said.

Pete chuckled. "Finish your steak, and I'll show you what *celebrate* means in Las Vegas!"

In her room, Elizabeth stared blankly at the open textbook on the desk in front of her. She was going to have a history test the following day and had been trying to study for the past two hours. But so far, she'd barely managed to read through a single page.

Elizabeth's thoughts kept drifting back to the

ugly scene between her brother and John Pfeifer in the *Oracle* office that afternoon. John's warning that Lila would destroy anyone who cared about her had been spoken with such conviction. Elizabeth braced her elbow on the desk and propped up her chin with her fist. *I don't know what to think anymore,* she realized. Most of all, Elizabeth worried about her brother. Watching him confront John Pfeifer had chilled her to the core. She had a feeling something terrible might happen to Steven if he became too caught up in Lila's problems.

Suddenly, the door of the bathroom that connected her room to Jessica's swung open, and what looked like a mountain of clothing with legs burst into the room.

Elizabeth snorted. "Jessica, are you in there?" she asked jokingly.

Jessica dumped her burden on Elizabeth's bed. "I'm trying to clear some walking space in my room," she said. "You don't mind if we keep these few things in your closet, do you?"

"No, I suppose not," Elizabeth said, then added in a sharper voice, "but hang them up yourself."

Jessica glared at her. "My, aren't we feeling rather bossy this evening!"

Elizabeth sighed wearily. "Jess, I'm really worried."

"OK, I'll hang them up," Jessica said.

Elizabeth rolled her eyes. "I'm worried about Lila," she clarified. "This whole ordeal with the fire, and the evidence against her . . ."

Jessica shrugged, as if she didn't care, and took some empty hangers out of Elizabeth's closet. "Lila can take care of Lila," she said flippantly.

Elizabeth knew her twin well enough to see right through her act. "What if Lila is really losing it?" Elizabeth asked.

Jessica turned to her and frowned. "What do you mean?"

Elizabeth got up and went over to help her sister. "Steven asked me to show him around the *Oracle* office this afternoon," she said. "He has it in his head that John Pfeifer started the fire."

Jessica's face turned pale, and her eyes widened with a look of alarm. "John Pfeifer," she murmured. "He is one creepy guy. And he certainly has a motive."

"Yeah, I suppose he does." Elizabeth slipped a blue lace top over a hanger and carried it over to the closet. "Anyway, John walked in on us while we were looking through his desk."

Jessica cringed. "What happened?"

"Steven challenged him head-on," Elizabeth told her. "He all but accused John of setting the Fowler Crest fire to try to get back at Lila. I felt like I was watching two gunslingers facing off in a hokey Western—except it was *real*."

"Do you think John did it?" Jessica asked.

"I don't know," Elizabeth replied. "But he said something . . ." She sat down on the edge of the bed and turned to her sister. "Jessica, before we left, John warned Steven that Lila is the type of girl who destroys those who care about her."

Jessica grimaced. "He's such a slime!"

"But what if there's some truth to it?" Elizabeth asked. "What if Lila really is out to destroy the people who care about her?"

"That's ridiculous," Jessica argued. "I can't believe you'd even listen to that total jerk."

Elizabeth began separating a tangle of silk tops. "Think about it, Jess. Remember back in middle school, when Lila went on a shoplifting spree to get back at her father?"

"That was years ago," Jessica argued. "But even if it wasn't, so what? Sure, Lila can be vindictive at times. She hates losing and not getting her own way. And she's spoiled. That doesn't make her criminally insane!"

Elizabeth sighed. "For the sake of argument," she began, "let's suppose—just suppose—John *didn't* try to rape Lila."

A look of rage flared up in Jessica's eyes. "If anyone is really losing it, it's you, Liz!"

128

Elizabeth held up her hands. "Just listen for a second," she pleaded. "What if John really cared about Lila, and she destroyed his life because of it? Then there was that counselor who tried to help her after the incident. He cared too—and Lila tried to destroy his reputation and career with a lie."

Elizabeth rose to her feet and paced nervously across her room, her thoughts churning. "And now the fire. Was Lila furious that her parents left her alone? Was that her way of trying to destroy them, by destroying what was theirs?"

Elizabeth sank down onto her chaise and pulled her knees up to her chest, wrapping her arms around her legs. "What if Lila is totally out of control?"

Jessica sighed wearily, her shoulders slumping. "I don't want any of this to be true," she whispered. "But . . ." She walked over to Elizabeth and sat down beside her. "If we're supposing, just supposing, I can add myself to that list of people who care about Lila. I feel like she's trying to hurt me by going out with Steven."

Elizabeth nodded. "I'm worried about him," she said. "He seems totally mesmerized by her. It's as if he's more concerned about proving Lila's innocence than he is about finding the truth."

Jessica shook her head. "Liz, I can't believe even for a second that Lila could be an arsonist.

Even as mad as I am at her, it just doesn't seem possible. For one thing, Lila loves Fowler Crest. And all that gasoline . . ." Jessica chuckled. "Lila loves her clothes. She wouldn't want to take the chance of ruining one of her precious outfits."

Elizabeth chewed the inside of her lower lip. "I wish I were as sure of Lila's innocence as you are," she said. "Maybe it's just that I'm so concerned for Steven."

"I'm just as concerned about him," Jessica replied. "I think Lila is using him and won't admit it, even to herself. But I'm positive she's not a criminal."

Elizabeth inhaled a deep breath and let it out slowly. "I hope you're right," she whispered.

"I think our biggest problem right now is this ridiculous romance between Lila and Steven," Jessica pointed out. "We have to figure out a way to bring them to their senses."

Elizabeth rolled her eyes. "Any suggestions?"

"I tried with Lila, and we ended up having a big fight," Jessica said.

"Ditto for me with Steven," Elizabeth added.

Jessica pressed her lips together and tilted her head. "Maybe . . . ," she began. Suddenly, she opened her eyes wide and grinned. "I have a great idea!"

"Let's hear it," Elizabeth said, skeptical.

"Lila is so possessive and demanding when it comes to boyfriends," Jessica pointed out. "If Steven were to neglect her a little, she'd be furious . . . and would start acting even *more* possessive and demanding."

"Steven would hate that!" Elizabeth added.

"So all you have to do is keep Steven busy this weekend," Jessica told her.

Elizabeth sighed. "You make it sound so easy, Jess. But I already tried that when we were attempting to cheer him up after the breakup with Billie. Steven kept ditching Todd and me—to be with Lila, as it turns out."

"We need a different approach. What if we tried to appeal to his big-brother side?" Jessica suggested. "You could tell him you desperately need his help with a school project. I know—say you have to interview him for an article that you've promised to do for the *Oracle*."

"That's not a bad idea," Elizabeth replied, thinking aloud. "I could actually write about his experiences at the D.A.'s office. I'll tell him I have to interview him this weekend because the article is due Monday morning."

"Is it a plan, then?" Jessica asked her.

"Yes," Elizabeth agreed. "Let's do it."

Jessica smiled brightly. "The Wakefield twins are back in action!" she exclaimed, flinging her fists into the air. "We're going to clean up this ugly liaison between Steven and Lila once and for all!"

Chapter 7

Seated next to his uncle at a blackjack table in the Starscape casino, Devon gazed at the cards lying faceup in front of him. He'd been dealt an ace, and then a queen. The queen was worth ten points, the ace was worth eleven. It was the highest possible score. If the dealer couldn't match it, Devon would double his thirty-dollar bet, plus fifteen more.

Devon was having a fabulous time. He and his uncle had been casino-hopping since after dinner. Pete was fun to watch. He was an ideal gambler. Always smiling, he kept a smooth look on his face at all times. His movements were efficient and confident. But Devon could see a sharp glint in his uncle's slate blue eyes, a trace of restlessness that the mask and expensive suit couldn't hide.

Pete clapped Devon on the back. "Not a bad hand, kid."

Devon shrugged. "I could win," he said mildly, copying his uncle's cool demeanor. But in his mind, he let out a wild cheer. *How long can my winning streak hold out?* Devon wondered excitedly. So far, he'd won at each casino, and had nearly tripled the cash he'd started with that evening.

Stifling a yawn, he tipped his head back and gazed up at the massive stained-glass dome ceiling. Lights shone through the glass, casting a reddish golden hue over the room. More lights shone at the top of the dome and along its bottom edge. *Vegas is definitely all about lights,* Devon thought, shaking his head. Wedged between the lights, he saw the glass circles of the closed-circuit TV monitors—the security system his uncle had referred to as the eye in the sky.

"Are you falling asleep on us, kid?" Pete asked.

"No way!" Devon said, turning his attention back to the game—and his fantastic hand.

· The elderly woman who sat on the other side of his uncle jumped to Devon's defense. Decked out in a fluorescent spandex jumpsuit, white fur stole, and tons of jewelry, she was as flashy and flamboyant as the casino itself.

"Now, Pete, don't you tease that boy while he's concentrating!" she cried in a shrill voice.

Everyone laughed. Even the dealer cracked a smile. Devon leaned forward slightly and turned to his champion. "Thanks, Mrs. Rumen," he said, giving her a big smile.

Pete rolled his eyes. "*Concentrating?* Ha! The kid's problem is that he has a short attention span," he said, laughing.

Mrs. Rumen wrinkled her nose at Pete, then blew Devon a kiss. "You're a good boy, Devon," she remarked.

Devon smiled to cover up his embarrassment. He still wasn't used to having older women fawn over him so blatantly. But he understood it was all in the spirit of fun, and he didn't want to hurt her feelings. "You're not so bad yourself," he replied.

Simpering, Mrs. Rumen patted her puffed-up silvery blond hair. Devon assumed it was bleached because her eyebrows were thick and dark. But the jewelry was genuine, and very expensive. Devon knew all about quality when it came to material things. He'd learned at a very young age. Luxury had been his mother's passion. *She would have been impressed with this lady's supply,* Devon thought irreverently. Even Mrs. Rumen's monogrammed lighter was solid gold and studded with diamonds.

Devon glanced at the other players sitting at

the semicircular table. Mrs. Rumen's daughter sat at the opposite end. Unlike her mother, Tina Rumen was very quiet, and conservatively dressed in a brown sweater and khaki pants. Devon guessed her age to be in the late twenties or early thirties. He also thought she looked a little embarrassed by her mother's gushing enthusiasm.

A middle-aged couple sat on Devon's other side. The husband reminded him of his old math teacher back in Connecticut. He didn't look like Mr. Isaacson, but he had the same ridiculous hairstyle—a few long strands wrapped across the shiny bald top. But he and his wife seemed to be nice people, and Devon did his best not to stare at the man's head.

The dealer passed more cards to the players who wanted a hit, or another card. Devon held his breath when his uncle's turn came up. Pete raised his finger once, then again . . . "Busted," he muttered as the dealer flipped over a three, four, six, and king. He'd gone over twenty-one, which meant an automatic loss. But his smile never wavered. "It's up to you now, kid. You'll have to defend the family honor," he joked.

"Devon is a very honorable boy," Mrs. Rumen chimed in, blowing him another kiss.

Tina Rumen cringed. "Mother, please!" she hissed, her face pinched with mortification.

"Oh, leave me alone," Mrs. Rumen bellowed, flicking her hand as if she were shooing away a pesky fly. "Devon and I have something going, don't we, sugar?"

Devon laughed. The setting was so bizarre anyway, he played along good-naturedly. "You bet we do, Mrs. R.," he responded evenly.

Pete nudged him in the ribs and gave him a sly wink. "What a ladies' man!" he teased.

Tina Rumen sent Devon a small, grateful smile. He returned the gesture, hoping to let her know that he wasn't taking her mother's outrageous flirting seriously.

Finally, it came time for the dealer to reveal his own hand. Devon felt his heart flutter as he watched the guy flip over his cards, revealing two sevens. He took another card—and went bust. Devon had won.

Pete slapped him on the back. "Way to go, kid!"

Devon bowed his head. "It was nothing," he said, his voice dripping with false modesty.

"I love you!" Mrs. Rumen declared, rushing over to envelop him in a huge, perfumed hug. "Let's get married."

Pete laughed heartily. Tina blushed to a shade of deep crimson.

Devon gently pulled himself out of Mrs. Rumen's arms. "Let's not rush into anything hasty."

Mrs. Rumen pinched his cheek. "You're such a doll! How I wish I were thirty—OK, *forty*—years younger."

"Mother, maybe we should go upstairs to our room and have a rest," Tina urged. "It's almost eight o'clock."

Devon frowned and glanced at his own watch to check out the time. *Seven-fifty* A.M.? he thought, totally astonished. *No wonder I'm yawning!* He and Pete had been gambling for close to twelve hours. But Pete didn't show any signs of fatigue at all.

Mrs. Rumen scooped up her chips and scowled at Tina. "How did I raise such a stodgy daughter?" she complained. "You're no fun at all." Then she stormed off toward the cashier's cage to cash in her chips.

Tina sighed noisily and gathered her things. She turned to go, then stopped and came over to Devon. "May I speak with you a second?" she whispered.

"Sure," Devon said, confused. Leaving his uncle at the table, he slowly walked with Tina toward the exchange counter.

"I'm sorry to take you away from the game," she began. "I just wanted to apologize for my mother . . . and thank you for being so gracious to her."

137

Devon shrugged. He didn't know what to say.

"She just got divorced," Tina explained.

"That could be rough, I suppose," Devon remarked.

Tina snorted. "It is rough—even though she's been through it five times before. You'd think she'd be used to the drill by now."

"Wow, you've had lots of fathers!" Devon blurted out. Immediately he regretted his words. "Sorry, that was a stupid thing to say. I didn't mean to be rude."

"I know you didn't. And for the record, I've had seven stepfathers," Tina said. "My mother was widowed a few times in between divorces."

Devon let out a low whistle. "How did you keep them straight when you were growing up?" he asked.

Tina's lips curved into a sad smile. "It wasn't easy. I suppose it's no mystery why I've never considered getting married."

Devon nodded. He knew what it was like to grow up with a messed-up family.

Tina stopped in her tracks and turned to Devon with her hand outstretched. "Anyway, thanks for being nice to my mom, Devon."

"No problem," he replied.

Just then, Mrs. Rumen came over to them, her brow creased with worry. "I can't find my room key," she complained, rummaging through her pink satin purse.

Tina rolled her eyes and draped her arm over her mother's shoulder. "You probably left it in the room," she said wearily. "But don't worry, I have mine."

Devon chuckled as they walked away.

"It was nice meeting you, Devon," Tina called to him over her shoulder. "If you're ever in Allentown, Pennsylvania, be sure to look us up."

"I will," Devon answered politely.

His uncle had just won a large stack of chips when Devon returned to the blackjack table. "Looks like your luck is picking up," Devon commented.

"Yours too, I see," Pete replied, winking overtly and nudging Devon in the ribs. "Although you're walking a dangerous path, kid."

"What are you talking about?" he asked, chuckling at his uncle's goofy antics.

Pete raised his eyebrows. "Going after the mother *and* the daughter? Isn't that a little greedy?"

Devon laughed. "They're both just using me to get to you," he joked.

Pete snickered and brushed his hand over his wavy hair. "Don't take it too hard," he teased. "I'm just better-looking than you are."

Devon nudged a few chips forward to bet on the next hand of cards. He realized a week had passed since he'd left Ohio. *That was one of the best decisions I've ever made,* he thought, mentally patting himself on the back. So far, no one in Vegas seemed to be out for his money—except for the casinos, of course. But they were up front and glaringly obvious about it. His uncle clearly didn't care if Devon was rich or poor.

Despite the tacky, hard-edged environment of the Las Vegas casino, Devon felt warm and cozy, as if he were wrapped in a soft blanket. *I do believe I've finally found a real home,* he thought.

Steven walked into his boss's office Friday morning, brimming with self-confidence. "I've uncovered some new evidence in the Fowler case," he announced as he handed Joe Garrison a manila folder containing the matching computer printouts. "I think you'll find it very interesting," Steven added.

"New evidence, huh?" Mr. Garrison muttered. He stubbed out his cigar and flipped open the folder.

Steven pulled a wooden chair closer to the desk and explained how the information from the Web page had mysteriously appeared in his box. "And this," he said, pointing to the sports article, "is something John Pfeifer was working on for the *Oracle,* Sweet Valley High's student newspaper. I found it on his desk in the *Oracle* office."

Steven sat back and eagerly waited for his boss to finish examining the papers. *It's all coming together*, he thought excitedly. *I've been an intern for only a few weeks, and already I've cracked the biggest arson case in Sweet Valley history!*

Mr. Garrison looked up with a dumbfounded expression on his face. "You consider this to be *evidence?*"

Steven's confidence sagged. It was hardly the congratulations he'd expected. "Well, yes . . . it shows the printouts came from the same—"

"It shows nothing!" Mr. Garrison bellowed, tossing the papers and the folder back at Steven.

Steven flinched, as if he'd been smacked in the face. His immediate impulse was to skulk out of the office and find somewhere to lick his wounds in private. But a hot surge of determination flared in his gut. *I know I'm right about John Pfeifer!* Steven thought.

Steven took a breath and let it out slowly. "Just let me explain my theory," he said, disciplining his voice to sound firm and in control.

Joe Garrison gave him a slight nod, though his expression remained as hard as stone.

"Notice how the print is skewed at the exact same angle on all of these pages," Steven pointed out. "I believe they all came from the same printer—the printer in the *Oracle* office."

"So what?" Mr. Garrison said. "Maybe someone

141

who works on the *Oracle* dropped off that profile to help you out with the case."

Steven shook his head. "Then why put it in my box anonymously?" he questioned. "No, I think the person who left this for me is trying to frame Lila."

Mr. Garrison glared at him incredulously. "That's quite a twist of logic, Wakefield."

Steven clenched his jaw, his frustration level surging higher. "I think someone planted the evidence against Lila at Fowler Crest and then sent me this profile because she fits some of the characteristics of the typical arsonist."

The D.A. stared at Steven for a long time, then glanced at the printouts again. "Even if your theory is right, it doesn't prove a thing."

"It proves there's a connection between the arsonist and the printer in the *Oracle* office," Steven argued.

Mr. Garrison raised one eyebrow. "The room is kept locked, right?"

"No," Steven replied, his voice sinking. "At least it wasn't locked yesterday afternoon when I was there."

"So anyone could have used that printer," Mr. Garrison remarked. "Any student, any teacher . . . anyone who wandered in from outside. Do you think we should investigate everyone who passes through the doors of the high school?"

Clearly defeated, Steven lowered his eyes and shook his head.

Mr. Garrison linked his hands behind his head and leaned back. "By the way, doesn't your sister work at the *Oracle*? Maybe she's the arsonist," he said mockingly.

Steven shifted uneasily. In his heart, he was pretty sure that John Pfeifer was the one who'd torched Fowler Crest. But he couldn't admit that to his boss without any solid evidence to back up his claim. *Something tells me my gut feelings won't impress Joe Garrison,* Steven thought wryly.

"Lila Fowler could've printed out that profile herself," Mr. Garrison continued. "Maybe she left it on your desk to throw you off. Maybe it's a cry for help and you can't see it because you're in way too deep."

"I'm not," Steven protested.

"Maybe you don't want to see what's right in front of your face!" Mr. Garrison accused.

Steven shook his head, his eyes wide. "That's not true."

Mr. Garrison bolted upright and leaned over the desk toward Steven. "Hear me loud and clear, Wakefield," he said in a cold, steely voice. "If you can't stay objective, you're off the case."

Shortly before noon, Devon dragged himself into the kitchen and headed straight for the coffeepot.

He heard his uncle moving around in the adjacent room, which was a combination pantry and laundry.

"Is that you, kid?" Pete called to him.

Devon sat down at the table and yawned. "Yeah, it's me," he replied sleepily.

The washing machine went on, and then Pete joined him in the kitchen. Devon was surprised how well rested and awake his uncle appeared. *It's going to take me a while to get used to partying all night long,* he thought, blinking in an attempt to wake himself up.

"Think you could run over to Linda's for me this afternoon?" Pete asked.

Devon grinned. "Sure," he answered. "What will it be this time? Candy? How about a poem?"

"How about this?" Pete said, removing a small square box from his shirt pocket.

"Another shiny trinket?" Devon asked, smirking.

"Hey, girls love sparkles," Pete said defensively as he slipped the box back into his pocket.

Devon sighed. "Fine, but we have to include something sentimental. That's the deal, right? We're moving to a multistrategy approach."

"This isn't a military operation," Pete countered jokingly. "I'm just trying to win back my woman."

Devon snorted. "Your *woman,*" he grunted. "How caveman!"

Pete raised his fists, flexing his muscles, and made

a goofy face. "Just call me macho man," he said.

Devon laughed. "I'd better get started on that love poem right now," he said, carrying his cup to the sink. "Because you need all the help you can get!"

"I'm absolutely *not* going to give Linda a sappy poem," Pete hollered after him.

A few hours later, Devon sat on Linda's pink couch and watched her open his uncle's latest gift. He knew Pete would quiz him later, so he tried to memorize the details of her reaction.

Linda removed the lid and set it down on the coffee table. Then she lifted a diamond-and-emerald bracelet from the box and draped it over her wrist. "This is nice," she said mildly.

Devon stared at the bracelet, his jaw hanging open. *That must have cost a fortune!* he thought.

Linda removed a folded slip of paper that was tucked under the bracelet. "What's this?" she asked, visibly intrigued.

Devon glanced over her shoulder and saw that it was his poem. *I guess Pete changed his mind,* he realized, trying to maintain a straight face. Devon held his breath as Linda read the poem.

When she looked up, her eyes were misty. "This is so beautiful," she said, her voice unsteady. "It's a love poem."

"And you like it?" Devon asked.

Linda sniffed. "Very much," she replied. "But there's no way you can make me believe Pete Whitelaw wrote it."

Devon turned his gaze to the window and the expansive view of the Strip. "Well, actually . . . the poem was written by . . ." He grinned. "My uncle's favorite poet—some obscure writer that no one's ever heard of."

Linda chuckled. "I never even knew Pete had a favorite poet," she said. "Your uncle is one surprise after another!"

Devon smiled triumphantly. "Can I tell him you said that?"

"I think he already knows," Linda replied.

Just then, a knock sounded on the door. Linda looked at her watch as she got up to answer. Devon noticed it wasn't the diamond watch his uncle had given her on Wednesday. She wasn't wearing any of the expensive gifts. *Linda obviously isn't the shiny-trinket type,* Devon realized. He only wished he could convince Pete to stop wasting his money and to approach Linda on his own.

"Come on in," he heard Linda tell the person at the door. Devon's eyes narrowed as she showed a distinguished-looking man with gray hair into the suite. She didn't bother to introduce him.

Who is this guy? Devon wondered. *Is he trying to make a move on Linda?*

146

The man glanced at Devon, then turned to Linda with a questioning look. "Am I early?" he asked.

"No, you're right on time," she replied. "Devon was just leaving, weren't you, dear?"

Devon slowly rose to his feet. "I guess so," he mumbled, catching her hint that it was time for him to go.

She looped her arm through his and walked him out of the suite.

In the hall, Devon hesitated. "Is there a message you want me to take back to Pete?"

"Nope," she answered.

"You're sure?" he asked.

Linda rolled her eyes. "*Good-bye,* Devon. And thank you so much for coming," she said, flashing him a huge smile—just before she shut the door in his face.

Devon felt uneasy as he walked away. He didn't like the idea of Linda entertaining some guy in her suite. Even though her relationship with the stranger hadn't appeared overly affectionate or romantic, Devon didn't think his uncle should take the chance of letting someone steal Linda away. *Pete better hurry up and get his act together—before it's too late,* Devon thought anxiously.

Chapter 8

Jessica was tempted to tear off a corner of her tuna sandwich and fling it across the table at Lila's head. *I wish that girl would shut up about my brother!* Jessica thought hotly. Lila hadn't stopped gushing since she'd sat down. Even the noisy clatter of the cafeteria couldn't drown out the sound of her irritating voice.

Jessica also wished Lila would eat her lunch somewhere else. After all, this was *supposed* to be the cheerleaders' table. Lila had always been included in the group only because she was Jessica's best friend. Now that the two of them were fighting, Lila didn't belong. *This table isn't big enough for both of us!* Jessica thought hotly. But she wasn't about to let herself be driven away.

"Steven is so *complex*," Lila was saying. "I keep

discovering something new about him every day."

Jessica bristled. *I will ignore her!* she resolved.

Amy Sutton narrowed her gray eyes in a pondering look. "Do you think that's because he's older?" she asked Lila.

No, it's because he's off his rocker, and so is Lila! Jessica retorted in her mind.

Lila's lips curled into a dreamy smile. "I'm sure his age has something to do with it. He's very mature. As well as just plain awesome!"

Annie Whitman smiled. "I think that's sweet, Lila."

Jessica thought it was *sick*.

Lila grinned. "Tonight we'll probably have a quiet evening, maybe heat up the leftovers we had last night, and then snuggle up to watch a video. But tomorrow night, Steven and I are going out on a real date."

"Where?" Sandra Bacon asked. The other girls were listening with rapt expressions.

"We have reservations at the Palomar House," Lila replied. "And then we're going to the Beach Disco."

Jessica gritted her teeth. The Palomar House was an incredible restaurant and the Beach Disco was a popular spot with the SVH crowd. She and Elizabeth would have to work very hard to prevent Steven from keeping this date with Lila.

"I've worked out a fabulous new cheerleading routine," Jessica announced abruptly, hoping to steer the conversation away from Lila and Steven. "I can't wait to show you guys at practice this afternoon."

"Wow, the Palomar House," Amy remarked, as if Jessica hadn't even spoken. "That's so fancy. I guess this means you and Steven are an official couple."

Lila giggled. "I think so."

Not if I have anything to say about it, Jessica thought fiercely.

Sitting at the next table, Caroline Pearce turned around, openly eavesdropping. "Who's going on a date to the Palomar House?" she asked.

"Steven Wakefield and Lila," Amy answered.

Jessica cringed. *Thanks a lot, Amy!* she raged inwardly. It was bad enough that Lila was fooling around with Steven. She didn't need to have Amy announce it in the cafeteria—and to Caroline Pearce, of all people! Caroline was the biggest gossip in Sweet Valley.

Jessica picked up her sandwich, then threw it back down on the tray. *I'm going to puke!* she thought.

Soon everyone would know about her brother and Lila, and even their date plans for Saturday night! SVH's gossip mill was more efficient than any of the cable news networks when it came to spreading a juicy story.

Hot, angry tears stung Jessica's eyes. She felt betrayed and humiliated beyond her limits. She couldn't take it anymore. Without a word to anyone at the table, she got up, dumped her lunch into the garbage bin, and stacked her tray.

Lila really is destroying my life! Jessica thought as she stormed out of the cafeteria.

Devon had arranged to meet his uncle for a late lunch at Kokomo's, which was located within the man-made rain forest in the Mirage Hotel's glass-domed atrium. The tables were topped with hut-like canopies, nestled between palm trees and exotic flowering bushes. Devon felt slightly disoriented—and amused—as he made his way through the lush tropical foliage to Pete's table.

"Las Vegas doesn't believe in doing things halfway, does it?" Devon quipped, raising his voice to be heard over the rushing sound of the waterfall.

Pete looked up anxiously. "How did it go?"

"Linda loved the poem," Devon announced.

Pete raised one eyebrow. "She did?"

"Absolutely," Devon replied smugly. "I thought she was going to cry."

"She probably thinks I've turned into a total sap," Pete grumbled, opening his menu.

"She thinks you're a surprising guy," Devon told him. "Her exact words were 'one surprise after another.'"

Pete glared at him over the top of the menu. "You didn't tell her I wrote that piece of garbage, did you?"

Devon pretended to be deeply insulted.

"Garbage?" he gasped, clutching his heart as if he'd been stabbed. "Linda said the poem was sweet."

Pete chuckled. "Yeah, like a rotting banana."

"Shows what you know! She made more of a fuss over that poem than she did over the bracelet," Devon boasted. "But to answer your question, I told her it was written by your favorite poet."

Pete tipped his head back and laughed. "You're too much, kid!"

Devon picked up his menu, then laid it back down on the table and leaned forward. "There is one thing you should know," he began haltingly. "A guy showed up at Linda's suite while I was there."

"Was he better-looking than me?" Pete asked flippantly as he opened his menu. "By the way, the crab cakes here are excellent."

Devon scowled at him. "Of course he was better-looking than you!" he retorted. "A mutant gorilla would be better-looking than you. And smarter too!"

Pete put his menu down and crossed his arms. "You think I should be worried about this guy?"

"Yeah!" Devon said sharply. "I can't say for sure what's going on between them. Linda didn't kiss him or anything like that, but still . . ."

Pete's expression became serious. "I hear you, kid," he said, nodding. "Linda is beautiful, smart, and classy. She's not the kind of woman who's likely to stay unattached for very long, is she?"

"That's why we have to step up your strategy," Devon insisted. "We can't take the chance of losing her to some other guy."

Pete sighed heavily. "Thank goodness you came along to help my case."

Devon shook his head. "You don't need me to be the go-between anymore. Linda's crazy about you, and I'm sure she'll see you now. You should deliver the next gift yourself."

Pete snorted and picked up his menu again. "She'd slam the door on me—after she spit in my face. She's done it before," he added.

"It's different now," Devon argued. "I've paved the way for you."

They put the conversation on hold when a waiter came over to take their lunch orders. Pete ordered the crab cakes and a mushroom salad. "I'll have the same," Devon said briskly. He was anxious to get back to the topic of his uncle's romance.

As soon as the waiter turned to go, Devon pounced. "You should see Linda's face whenever I mention your name," he told Pete. "Her eyes get all glassy, and she tries not to smile. . . ."

Pete rubbed his hand over his chin. "You've made a good start, I'll grant you that much. But paving the way is going to take more time. You have no idea how heated—and *ugly*—our breakup was." His gaze flickered to the side. "We both said some terrible things."

Devon exhaled sharply. "It's time to put all that behind you and start over."

"Maybe in a few weeks," Pete said.

Devon stared at his uncle, noting the nervous look in his eyes. "You're scared, aren't you?" he challenged.

Pete nodded. "Terrified."

Devon shook his head woefully. His uncle seemed so competent and sure of himself. *How can a woman turn a guy like him into a total wimp?* Devon wondered. *And how on earth can he afford to shower Linda with such expensive gifts?*

"You're not going to bail out on me, are you?" Pete asked.

Devon sighed heavily. "No, of course not. I'll keep playing this game until you win Linda over— or until you declare bankruptcy."

Pete's eyebrows shot up in a look of astonished disbelief. "Bankruptcy?" he uttered, sounding amused.

"Yeah, *bankruptcy*," Devon said. "Today's little gift is probably worth somewhere between twelve and thirteen thousand. That's not counting my poem, of course. You can't put a price on literary genius."

Pete chuckled. "You think highly of yourself, Mr. Literary Genius. I like that in a person."

"Yesterday's necklace was in the twenty-thousand range," Devon continued.

Pete nodded. "Very impressive. You're right on target with both estimates. Isn't there a game show where we can cash in on this extraordinary talent of yours?" he teased.

Devon ignored the jibe. "How long can you keep giving Linda such expensive daily gifts?" he asked, concerned.

"I shop the sales," Pete responded dryly.

It started to rain just as Elizabeth and her boyfriend, Todd Wilkins, pulled into the parking lot of the Dairi Burger that evening. Heavy drops pounded on the roof of Todd's BMW and thick sheets of water cascaded over the windshield.

"It's really pouring!" Elizabeth exclaimed. A thin streak of lightning flashed in the sky, followed by a loud clap of thunder.

Todd turned off the engine and pocketed the keys. "We could stay put and wait until it stops," he said, reaching over to stroke a lock of her hair between his fingers.

Elizabeth flashed him a coy smile. Although they'd been dating each other for ages, she still considered Todd to be the most exciting guy at Sweet Valley High. He also happened to be gorgeous, with a tall, athletic build, wavy brown hair, broad shoulders, and an easy smile. "You don't think we'd get bored just sitting in your car?" she teased.

"I've got some ideas about how we might prevent

that," he said, curving his hand around the back of her neck.

Elizabeth saw the shimmering passion in his warm brown eyes as he gently drew her toward him. "I'll bet you've got ideas," she murmured, her heart picking up speed. A delightful rush of sensations tingled up and down her spine.

Todd touched his lips to hers. "Great ideas," he whispered.

Closing her eyes, Elizabeth let out a soft moan. She wrapped her arms around Todd's lean waist and deepened the kiss. The rain, the Dairi Burger, the other cars in the parking lot . . . everything seemed to fade away in the sweet sensation of the moment.

Suddenly, Todd's stomach growled, breaking the romantic spell. "What rotten timing," he said sheepishly.

Elizabeth laughed. "I think it's time for your feeding," she teased. "We can get back to your *great ideas* later tonight."

Todd gave her a quick kiss. "Sounds like a plan!"

Holding hands, they dashed through the rain to the entrance of the Dairi Burger. As was usual for a Friday night, the place was crowded. Elizabeth waved to her twin, who was sitting at a table near the door with some of the other cheerleaders.

Winston Egbert and Maria Santelli invited

Todd and Elizabeth to sit with them. Without even looking at each other, Elizabeth and Todd both answered at the same time with an emphatic "No thanks." All four of them cracked up.

"I get the message," Winston said. He and Maria were good friends with both Todd and Elizabeth, and lots of fun. But Elizabeth wanted to be alone with Todd, and she was pleased to see that he felt the same way.

Most of the booths were taken, but Elizabeth spotted an empty one way in the back corner, and she and Todd headed straight for it.

"Alone at last," Todd muttered as he folded his lean, six-foot-plus frame into the booth and reached across the table for Elizabeth's hands.

As if on cue, Jessica rushed over and plunked herself down next to Elizabeth. "I agree with you one hundred percent," Jessica said. "She *is* out to destroy me."

Todd and Elizabeth exchanged bemused looks.

"And I'm not going to let her get away with it," Jessica added.

Elizabeth sighed heavily. "Jess, can't this wait until later? I'm on a date."

Jessica bristled. "A *real* date, she says. Lila is going around telling everyone that she and Steven are going out on a *real* date tomorrow! How can our own brother be so . . . so . . . *wacko?*"

"Runs in the family," Todd mumbled. Trying not to laugh, Elizabeth narrowed her eyes and scowled at him.

"Lila is such a traitor," Jessica spat. "And the rest of my friends aren't a whole lot better! They all think it's just fine for Steven and Lila to be seeing each other. Amy, Annie, and Sandra are sitting over there right now, talking about what a cute couple they make! What happened to support and loyalty among friends?"

Elizabeth nodded sympathetically, although she never considered her twin's friends to be very reliable. Most of them seemed shallow, self-centered, and fiercely competitive with each other.

And besides, they're Lila's friends too, Elizabeth added silently. Even if they wanted to be loyal and supportive, they couldn't side with both Lila *and* Jessica.

Todd turned Elizabeth's hand over and glanced at her wristwatch. Elizabeth shifted uneasily and rolled her eyes, sending him a secret plea for patience.

"The whole school knows about them by now," Jessica grumbled.

"We'll take care of it," Elizabeth murmured gently. "But later, OK? Right now, um . . . Todd and I would like to be alone."

Jessica stared at her. "I just remembered. You

were supposed to keep Steven at home tonight," she said. "What are you doing here?"

Todd exhaled sharply, clearly annoyed. "I'm going to check out the video games for a while."

Elizabeth sent him a pained I'm-sorry smile as he slipped out of the booth.

"Steven is probably with Lila right now, heating up leftovers!" Jessica continued, her voice shaking with anger. "And it's all your fault!"

Elizabeth stiffened and slowly counted to ten under her breath. "Jess, I don't like what's going on between Lila and Steven any more than you do. But getting all worked up about it isn't going to help," she said, keeping her voice level—even though she was quickly losing her patience. "And for your information, Steven is not with Lila. He's working late tonight."

"Are you sure?" Jessica asked.

"Yes, I'm sure," Elizabeth retorted. "I called him at the D.A.'s office and told him I needed his help for the *Oracle* piece. He said he had tons of work to do and wouldn't be home until close to midnight."

Jessica's expression brightened. "That'll work just as well," she said. "Lila isn't the type to be impressed by hard work, especially if it causes her to be stuck at home by herself on a Friday night."

"I'll ask him to help me with the article tomorrow,"

Elizabeth thought aloud. "With any luck, we won't get it done too quickly."

Jessica snickered. "I'll figure out something I can need our big brother for too," she added. "By the sound of Lila's bragging, I get the impression that their date at the Palomar House is a big deal—although she does tend to exaggerate."

"I heard all about it too—although the gossip network seemed a little slow today," Elizabeth remarked wryly. "The news didn't reach me until seventh period."

"Maybe we should call Billie," Jessica suggested.

"And tell her what?" Elizabeth asked. "The way Steven tells it, *she* broke up with *him* because he accepted the internship at the D.A.'s office without talking it over with her first. I doubt there's anything we can say to correct the problem. I just hope they can work things out and get back together."

Jessica shrugged. "Let's offer her a bribe to take him back."

Elizabeth rolled her eyes. "Brilliant, Jess," she replied sarcastically. "Why don't you take up a collection right here . . . and let me get back to my date with Todd!"

Chapter 9

Saturday evening, Devon browsed through the various shops in the lobby of the Starscape Hotel. The ones in the Luxor, Excalibur, and Tropicana hadn't offered anything exciting. He was on his way to see Linda again, and wanted to find something unique and romantic to give her. Of course, Pete's contribution to the cause was already in Devon's pocket—a small wrapped package that probably contained another expensive bauble.

Devon found a CD of romantic ballads, which he thought would make a perfect gift for Linda. In the candy shop next to the record store, he bought a heart-shaped box of chocolate truffles. *We have to beat the competition,* Devon decided. He was still worried about the man who'd shown up at Linda's suite the previous day.

As Devon passed through the casino on his way out of the Starscape, he ran into Mrs. Rumen and her daughter, who were headed in the opposite direction.

"How's it going?" Devon called to them politely.

Mrs. Rumen burst into tears.

Startled, Devon stopped in his tracks and gaped at the two of them. Tina's expression was grave, her skin pale. And Mrs. Rumen appeared to have aged twenty years since he'd last seen her.

"What happened?" he asked.

"We were robbed," Tina told him. "Someone cleaned out our hotel suite this morning while we were out having breakfast. They took everything—cash, jewelry, our camera. . . ."

Devon frowned.

"That's terrible! How did they get in?"

"They probably used my own key," Mrs. Rumen sobbed. "I'm such a foolish old woman. I never should have come here!"

Tina shook her head.

"It's as much my fault. My mother hasn't been able to find her hotel key for the past few days," she explained to Devon. "I should have reported it, but I just assumed she'd misplaced it somewhere in the suite. Now I think someone might have stolen it right out of her purse."

Devon was outraged and disgusted. *A guy would*

have to be a serious creep to do something so low, he thought.

"You reported the robbery to the police, right?"

"We just got back from the police station. We've been filling out reports all morning," Tina said with a slight nod.

"Do they have any leads?" Devon asked.

"Nothing definite," Tina answered glumly. "But they told us there's been a sudden increase in hotel burglaries over the past few months, and they're aggressively investigating that. They think a circle of organized thieves is at work in the area."

Mrs. Rumen dabbed her eyes with a lace handkerchief.

"We should have been warned about this before we booked our vacation," she said.

"I agree," Devon replied. "Anyway, I hope they catch them soon."

"Thanks, Devon," Tina said, smiling sadly. "I'm glad we got a chance to say good-bye to you."

"You're leaving Vegas, then?" he asked.

"As soon as possible," Tina replied emphatically.

Mrs. Rumen sniffed. "You should get out of here too," she warned Devon. "This is an awful place. No one should have to stay here."

Devon continued thinking about Mrs. Rumen's predicament as he left the Starscape.

"A hotel robbery—what rotten luck!" he muttered under his breath. He'd been having so much fun over the past week that he'd stopped noticing the seedier side of Las Vegas.

But now, as Devon walked along the Strip, everything seemed tacky and depressing. It was a place where the rich had fun and the poor had misery. Again, he worried about the steady stream of expensive gifts he'd been delivering to Linda, and about the amount of money his uncle seemed to be spending on her.

Devon recalled Pete's brush-off when he'd tried to raise the issue at Kokomo's the day before. "I shop the sales," his uncle had said.

What does that mean? Devon wondered. Even more puzzling was Pete's insistence that the gifts continue for a few more weeks.

Devon sidestepped a mob of tourists who were gawking at the hokey volcano in front of the Mirage. *Stolen jewelry would probably cost a lot less, wouldn't it?* he reasoned.

When he reached the Brada Hotel, Devon hesitated. Standing on the street outside the main entrance, he gazed up at the sleek glass tower ribboned with pink and yellow tubes of neon lights. Linda's suite was way up in the top left corner of the building.

Is my uncle buying hot *jewelry for her?* Devon

asked himself. That would mean Pete was supporting the criminals who'd burglarized the Rumens that morning.

Devon felt a gnawing, twisting sensation in his gut. He hated himself for suspecting his uncle. Pete was the first person who'd taken an interest in him in years. They were family. *Some loyal nephew I turned out to be!* Devon thought, giving himself a swift mental kick in the head.

Devon pushed himself forward and entered the hotel. But he found he couldn't shake his doubts about the expensive gifts he'd been delivering every day. He slipped his hand into the pocket of his suit jacket and removed the small box Pete had given him that afternoon. Devon wondered how expensive this one was, and whether it equaled the exorbitant value of Pete's other gifts to Linda.

Devon was still clutching the package in his hand as he rode the elevator up to the penthouse floor. He felt guilty for suspecting his uncle, but he couldn't stop himself. He set the bag containing the CD and candy on the carpeted floor of the elevator, and unwrapped the gift from Pete.

The small red cardboard box was taped shut. Devon impatiently ripped off the sticky tape, peeling off strips of the red color with it. The box was covered with white, papery slashes by the time he yanked off the lid and tossed it on the floor.

Inside the box, resting on a wad of white tissue paper, was a solid gold cigarette lighter. Devon's heart skipped a beat. His hand shaking, he picked up the lighter and held it in his open palm. It felt cool to the touch, and heavy for its size. Then he flipped it over, and saw the swirling *R* monogram circled with diamond chips—the same design he'd noticed on Mrs. Rumen's lighter the night before she'd been robbed.

Devon jerked back, dropping the lighter as if it had suddenly turned into a poisonous snake. *Maybe it's a coincidence,* a small, hopeful voice in his mind piped up.

Pressing his back against the paneled wall of the elevator, Devon sank to the floor. He desperately wanted to believe it wasn't Mrs. Rumen's lighter, but the logic was too far-fetched.

Devon's mind was flooded with one ugly suspicion after another. *Did Pete buy it stolen . . . or did he steal it himself?* Devon picked up the lighter again and squeezed it in his fist. He remembered he'd been talking with Tina when her mother had come over to complain that she'd lost her room key. *Did Pete take Mrs. Rumen's key out of her bag at the blackjack table?* he wondered.

The elevator stopped at the ninth floor for an elderly woman. She glanced at Devon sitting on the floor and hesitated, clearly nervous about sharing an elevator with him.

Devon rose to his feet and gave her a reassuring smile.

"I was just resting," he murmured sheepishly.

That seemed to satisfy her. She stepped into the elevator and punched in a floor number on the panel.

"I didn't mean to offend you," she said to Devon. "It's just that a woman alone . . . well, you can't be too careful these days."

Devon rolled his eyes.

"Tell me about it," he muttered. He thought about Mrs. Rumen and Tina finding their room burglarized—courtesy of his uncle Pete.

What if I'm totally wrong about all this? Devon asked himself silently. He racked his brain to come up with a reasonable explanation for the gold lighter in his hand. *Maybe it's a popular design, and the R stands for the designer, not Rumen. . . .*

"Is this yours?" the woman asked, startling him. She was holding up his shopping bag. "I found it on the floor."

Devon blinked. "Yes, thanks," he said, taking it from her.

Her eyes narrowed. "Are you OK, young man?"

"I'm fine," he replied.

"You look as if you've lost your best friend," she remarked.

Devon uttered a humorless chuckle. *Close,* he answered silently.

He rubbed his thumb over the gold lighter as he watched the progression of floor numbers on the panel above the door. In a few moments, he would be arriving at Linda's suite.

Devon was determined to find out what was going on, no matter how much the truth might hurt.

Sitting on the couch in the pool house, Lila glared at the clock on the opposite wall. Steven was twenty minutes late. *Where is he?* she wondered.

Lila was anxious to hear about Steven's progress on the arson case. She didn't know when all the details would be totally resolved, but she was sure Steven would take care of everything as quickly as possible. Lila just wanted to hear him tell her once and for all that she was no longer under suspicion of setting her house on fire.

"It'll all be over soon," she whispered reassuringly. She was positive her life would be back to normal at last. She and Steven deserved to celebrate. But if he didn't arrive soon, they would miss their dinner reservation at the Palomar House.

Lila crossed her arms, her lips pursed tightly. *She* had spent the entire day preparing for this date. It had taken hours of searching through the shops at the Valley Mall to find the perfect outfit and accessories. And then she'd spent a few more hours at the Silver Door, the most exclusive beauty salon in Sweet Valley, getting a manicure, facial, and conditioning treatment for her hair.

Lila stopped in front of the window and looked at her reflection in the glass. She'd felt like a princess when she'd gotten dressed that evening. The pale green satin sheath had been an inspired choice, and the exquisite emerald earrings she had bought at Stowe's complemented it perfectly.

Steven had better not stand me up again tonight! she thought, fuming. She'd spent the previous evening waiting for him to show up. Finally, he'd called her around ten P.M. to tell her he wouldn't be coming.

Lila plunked herself down on the couch again. Glancing at the clock, she realized that they'd just missed their reservation at the Palomar House.

"That's just great," she muttered sarcastically.

She reached for the cordless phone on the side table and punched in the Wakefields' number. Jessica answered on the first ring.

Hearing her voice, Lila bristled.

"Is Steven there?" she asked, keeping her tone extremely cool. She still hadn't forgiven Jessica for her lack of support and for the horrible things she'd said about Lila's relationship with Steven.

"I really don't know where he is," Jessica replied, sounding just as cool. "He might have gone back to SVU for the weekend." She paused, then added, "Maybe he's staying at his *apartment*."

Lila's blood boiled. She could imagine Jessica's smug expression as she delivered that bit of news. Steven had shared his apartment at SVU with Billie Winkler, his former girlfriend, and Jessica was obviously trying to imply that they might be getting back together. Lila didn't believe it for an instant.

Lila disconnected the call and began pacing again. Steven was tardy, but he wasn't cruel.

Jessica was cruel.

I wish that girl were here right now! Lila thought, clenching her right hand into a fist. She would have loved to smash it right into Jessica's nose.

A moment later, the phone rang again. It was Steven. "Lila, can you come pick me up?" he asked.

Lila frowned. "Where are you?"

"At home," he replied.

"Really?" Lila turned to the window and smirked at her reflection. "You're not leaving for SVU, then?"

There was a pause on the line.

"No," he said at last. "We have a date tonight, remember?"

Lila chuckled. "Yes, of course I do. I'll be right over."

"I'll be waiting for you in the front yard," Steven told her. "I've already called the Palomar House. They're holding our table for an extra fifteen minutes. If we hurry, we can still make it."

Grinning, Lila clicked off the phone and grabbed her jeweled evening bag. *Wait till I get my hands on that Jessica!* she thought.

"Sorry for the mix-up," Steven said as he hopped into Lila's green Triumph convertible.

Lila gave him a big smile.

"That's OK, I don't mind driving. Is something wrong with your Volkswagen?" she asked, then added, "Maybe you should think about trading it in for a newer car."

Steven clenched his jaw. He'd just spent two of the must frustrating days he could remember. The previous day's meeting with the D.A. had been just the beginning. Mr. Garrison had insisted Steven attend a series of meetings with other investigators working on the Fowler Crest case, and it seemed everyone was convinced that Lila was guilty. Steven had also been stuck with all of the research assignments, and had spent his Friday night sitting in front of a computer in the D.A.'s office.

"I don't need a new car," Steven replied tersely. "I just couldn't find my keys."

Lila glanced at him sideways and giggled.

"Don't you have a spare set to keep for emergencies?" she asked, pushing her hair back from her face.

"I couldn't find them either." Steven glanced at the passing scenery as they headed down Calico Drive. The evening was warm and balmy, perfect for riding in an open convertible. Steven leaned back and tried to relax as he stared up at the night sky.

He had looked forward to spending a much-deserved peaceful Saturday at home. But his sisters had ruined that for him. Elizabeth had hounded him all day for an interview about his internship—exactly what Steven hadn't wanted to think about for the time being. And Jessica had been acting just plain weird—begging him to help her rearrange the furniture in her room, fix her broken CD player, and discuss her sudden aspiration to attend law school.

Then, when it had been time to leave for his date, Steven hadn't been able to find his car keys. He was sure he'd left them on his dresser in his bedroom. And it had been strange that the second set he kept in his top drawer had been missing too.

"Come on, Steven," Lila said, squeezing his arm. "Don't keep me hanging. Tell me!"

Steven stiffened. He knew what Lila wanted to hear. But he dreaded having to tell her that they had nothing to celebrate after all.

"My investigation isn't over yet," he replied, hedging.

"What did the D.A. think about your evidence against John Pfeifer?" she asked.

Steven leaned his head back and stared up at the sky. "He wasn't impressed."

Lila caught her bottom lip between her teeth and kept her gaze forward. "What exactly does that mean?" she asked softly.

"He said that even if the Web page information had been printed out in the *Oracle* office, it didn't necessarily prove anything about John Pfeifer," Steven told her. "The file could've been downloaded by anyone."

"So I'm still the number-one suspect. That's just great," Lila muttered sarcastically.

Steven winced, as if she'd slapped him. "I tried, Lila. And I'll keep trying."

Lila shrugged. "Sure, whatever."

They drove the rest of the way to the Palomar House in stony silence. Steven had felt disappointed enough without the added burden of Lila's sullen attitude. But he quickly chastised himself for feeling resentful toward her. *It's her reputation—and maybe her freedom—that is on the line,* Steven reminded himself.

As they walked across the parking lot toward the front entrance of the restaurant, Steven reached for Lila's hand.

"I'm sorry it didn't work out like I'd hoped," he told her.

"Me too," Lila grumbled.

Steven loosely draped his arm across her shoulders. "Let's try to make the best of this evening," he suggested. "You look very nice, by the way."

Lila looked up at him with a bland expression and said, "Thanks."

A few minutes later, Steven and Lila were seated at a small table in the Palomar House's elegant dining room. The strains of piped-in violin music could be heard over the hum of muted conversations and the clinking of silverware and china.

"This is really nice," Steven said, trying to sound cheerful.

"*Lovely*," Lila responded in an icy tone.

Steven reached across the table and squeezed her hand. "Lila, I'm not giving up."

Lila glanced at their joined hands, then looked up at his face. "Is that why you ditched me last night?" she asked pointedly.

"I had to work late. But I did call you to let you know," he added defensively.

Lila pulled back her hand. "Yeah, around ten o'clock, wasn't it?"

Steven felt as if he was being tested by both Lila and his boss, and he hated it. "I lost track of time."

A waiter came over to take their order. "We're not ready," Steven told him. They hadn't even opened their menus.

"We have several specials this evening," the waiter informed them, and immediately began to recite a long litany of various appetizers, entrees, and desserts, including their ingredients. Steven clenched his fists under the table as the guy went on and on with barely a pause.

Finally the waiter finished his drawn-out recitation and left Steven and Lila alone.

"The sautéed scallops with morel mushrooms sound interesting, don't you think?" Lila remarked. "At least we'll get a decent meal out of this date."

Steven exhaled heavily. "Lila, I know you're disappointed about the way things turned out. So am I. But please try to understand. My job is in jeopardy. I have to prove myself all over again, or they'll never take me seriously."

Lila sniffed. "Because of me?"

"Well, yeah," Steven answered truthfully. "Mr. Garrison believes my relationship with you is compromising my objectivity."

"Oh, I get it!" Lila snapped. "You're going to tell me very politely that you think we should cool it for a while. Just when I need you most, you're going to take a hike."

"No, that's not what I mean," Steven countered.

Lila raised her chin. "Don't worry, Steven," she said, her brown eyes brimming with tears. "I'm used to being abandoned. It's the story of my life."

"Lila, that's not what I'm saying! I don't want to stop seeing you," Steven insisted. "We just have to be discreet, that's all."

A tear slipped down Lila's cheek. "In other words, you shouldn't be seen with me because it might hurt your precious career?"

Steven's stomach twisted painfully. But he couldn't deny her words.

Lila wiped her tear away with the back of her hand. "Gee, Steven. Maybe I should have worn a paper bag over my head, so no one would know you're having dinner with a suspected criminal tonight," she said sarcastically.

"Tonight is OK," Steven replied lamely.

"But never again, right?" Lila asked, raising her voice.

Steven looked around nervously, noting a few curious glances from the other diners.

"What do you want from me, Lila?" he asked desperately. "I'm doing the best I can."

"Well, so am I!" she spat back at him. "But apparently that's not good enough for you!"

"That's not true, and I think you know that," Steven replied.

Lila pushed back her chair and stood up. "I don't know what I know anymore," she responded tightly.

"Where are you going?" Steven asked.

Lila glared at him. "To the ladies' room, if that's OK with you." With that, she stormed off, her head high and her shoulders squared.

Steven flipped open his menu and accidentally knocked over his water glass.

"Perfect," he mumbled sarcastically as he wiped up the spill with his napkin. It seemed nothing was working out lately, despite his good intentions.

Steven absently traced patterns on the damp tablecloth with his spoon. *I don't know what to do next,* he realized. Mr. Garrison had all but forbidden him to spend time pursuing other leads in the arson case. But as important as his internship was, Steven still felt obligated to help Lila clear her name.

Suddenly, a loud crash of broken glass startled Steven. From the corner of his eye, he caught a glimpse of a small object falling through a gaping hole in the window. It landed on the floor and exploded in a flash of light.

Steven's heart jumped to his throat. The dining room erupted in chaos. Flames engulfed the curtains and began to spread across the carpeted floor. People were screaming and running frantically to the exits.

Lila! Steven thought, gripped with panic as he pushed his way toward the corridor where the rest rooms were located. Suddenly, the restaurant's fire sprinklers went on, instantly drenching the entire dining room and everyone in it. The screams rose to a deafening pitch.

Steven wiped the water out of his eyes, barely aware that he was soaked to the skin. His only thought was to find Lila. He yelled her name, but his voice was drowned out by the frantic commotion.

Sitting in a pink cushioned chair in Linda's hotel suite, Devon watched as she sank her teeth into a chocolate truffle.

"Mmm," she murmured, closing her eyes. "Utterly fabulous!"

Devon shifted uneasily. His stomach felt as if it were tied in knots, and his heart was pounding like a kettledrum. "Glad you like them," he responded automatically.

Linda grinned. "I do," she replied, holding the box out to him. "Try one, Devon."

Devon shook his head. He didn't think he could swallow anything, let alone keep it down.

"I love this CD too," Linda said, picking it up from the coffee table where she'd placed it earlier. "Romantic music, chocolates . . ." She smiled dreamily. "Your uncle is trying to spoil me, isn't he?"

"I think that's the idea," Devon said, silently adding, *Even if it means stealing from nice old ladies to do it*.

Linda chuckled and peered inside the paper bag the presents had been in. "Is there anything

178

else Pete wanted you to give me?" she asked in a deceptively casual tone.

Devon looked her straight in the eye and shook his head.

Linda's smile began to sag. "Are you sure?"

"Yes, I'm sure," Devon replied evenly.

"But there must be something else," Linda insisted.

Devon sat back, bracing his elbows on the arms of the chair. "That's all there is," he lied.

The lines around Linda's mouth deepened as her face grew hard. Her dark eyes glimmered like two pieces of black ice. At that instant, Devon felt as if a curtain had ripped open in his mind, forcing him to stare at the cold truth. His heart froze, his throat tightened, and his eyes stung.

Linda and Pete are in on something together, Devon thought. *And I've been used—again.* For one horrifying moment, he was afraid he might break down into tears.

Devon swallowed thickly and drew in a deep breath. "So what is this all about?" he asked, his voice low and chilly. "I've already figured out that the stuff I've been passing to you is hot. Maybe you'd be nice enough to fill me in on the details?"

"Looks like you've got your mind made up already," Linda said defensively.

Devon snorted. "You and my uncle are nothing but a couple of low-life crooks."

Linda crumpled up the bag and pitched it across the room. "What gives you the right to judge us?"

"I'm the delivery boy!" Devon retorted. "I have a right to know about the stolen merchandise I've been carrying around for the past week."

"Go home and ask your uncle," Linda snapped.

"My uncle." Devon let out a bitter laugh. "What a sap I've been, shopping for sentimental gifts and writing poems in the name of love. . . ."

"What do you mean?" Linda asked sharply.

"This ridiculous performance we've been acting out," Devon said disdainfully. "Except I didn't know it was make-believe. I thought Pete really wanted to win you back, and I knocked myself out trying to help him."

Linda's face paled. "You mean all the other gifts—the flowers, the candy . . . that wonderful poem—they weren't from Pete?"

"The show's over, Linda," Devon said. "You can get off the stage now."

Linda got up and walked over to the window. "It's not an act . . . not completely," she said. "I've been in love with Pete for a long time. When he started sending romantic gifts, I assumed it meant he was falling for me too."

"They were my idea," Devon told her, wanting to lash out at her.

Linda whirled around and stared at him. "I

guess Pete was just softening me up to keep me fencing his stolen goods."

Devon raised his eyebrows. "You're his fence. How convenient."

"Not really," Linda spat. "The police were starting to get wise to us. I was being watched."

So this is the circle of thieves, Devon realized, recalling what Tina had told him of the police's ongoing investigation.

"It was getting too dangerous for Pete to pass the loot off to me directly," Linda explained.

Devon sneered. "And in walks Pete's dumb nephew from Connecticut. Lucky break, huh?"

Linda shrugged. "You provided a short-term solution."

"Until they link my uncle to me, and me to you," Devon replied.

Linda came over and sat back down on the couch.

"We only needed a few more good scores and then we could both retire. Actually, I was going to quit a while back, but Pete convinced me to stay on for just a bit longer." She lowered her eyes. "I did it for him, hoping . . ."

"That he'd fall madly in love with you?" Devon asked snidely.

Linda shot him a dirty look. "I'm not thrilled with this arrangement either," she shouted. "I hate

181

living on the edge, constantly looking over my shoulder. You don't know how many times I've been tempted to leave this stinking town and move back home."

"But you didn't, because of my dear, sweet uncle?" Devon guessed.

Linda's eyes filled with tears. "That's right. But now I see that he's been using me all along."

Devon shrugged. "That's my opinion too."

Linda sniffed. "Like I told you, Devon. Your uncle cares about no one but himself."

"I should've listened," Devon whispered.

Linda got up and pushed her hair back from her face. "Wait here," she told Devon. She left the room and returned a few minutes later with a large grocery bag.

"Take this junk to Pete," she said, plunking the bag down at Devon's feet. "Let him do his own dirty work. And tell him I'm leaving. I'm going home!"

Devon got up and grabbed the bag. Linda was already on the phone, calling for a taxi to take her to the airport. Devon gave her a long, hard look. He saw the tears streaming down her face, the anguish in her eyes. But Devon felt no sympathy for her. Just cold anger.

Chapter 10

Devon stood at the door of his uncle's apartment and let the bag of stolen goods drop to the floor. The hopes he'd had only a week ago, when he'd first arrived, came back to him now, torturing him. *A real family at last,* Devon taunted himself silently. *When will I ever learn?* He picked up the bag and opened the door.

Pete was standing in front of the mirror in the living room, adjusting his necktie. "How'd it go, kid?" he asked cheerfully. "I'm on my way out for the evening, but I left you a few bucks on the coffee table."

Devon didn't say a word. He glanced at the three hundred-dollar bills on the coffee table and almost laughed. *Am I supposed to be impressed?* he thought bitterly.

"I'm playing high-stakes baccarat at the Tropicana," Pete continued. "But maybe we can grab a bite later."

Devon responded by dumping the contents of the bag on the coffee table.

That got Pete's attention. "What's going on?" he asked, staring at the pile of jewelry cases and small boxes.

Devon placed the diamond-studded gold cigarette lighter on top of the mound. "That's what I was wondering. But now I know."

Pete picked up the lighter and slipped it into his pocket. "You figured it out, huh?"

"Most of it," Devon replied. "Linda filled me in on the fine points."

Pete nodded, his expression drawn. "What's next? Are you going to turn us over to the police?"

Devon snorted. "Believe me, it's tempting. But I'm going to let you slip up on your own. Call it family loyalty," he spat. "Besides, I don't want to stay in this miserable town for one minute more than I have to."

Devon turned his back on his uncle and walked calmly to the bedroom he'd been using. He changed into a pair of his own blue jeans and a black T-shirt, then balled up his borrowed Armani suit and threw it across the room. It landed in a heap on the floor. Devon stared at it for a long moment, totally disgusted. *Now I know how my uncle can afford to buy those fancy Italian suits*, he thought.

Pete walked in a moment later, as Devon was packing his things. He glanced at the clothes on the floor, then at Devon. "I guess you're pretty mad, huh?"

Devon clenched his jaw and said nothing as he threw a pile of socks into his bag.

"You don't have to leave because of this," Pete said. "Linda and I can find someone else to be our go-between."

Devon glared at him. "Linda's gone . . . just like I'm going to be in a few minutes."

Pete's lips flickered in a nervous smile. "What are you talking about, kid? Linda's gone *where?*"

"Home," Devon said.

"Home?" Pete echoed, sinking down to a sitting position on the edge of the bed. "What do you mean?"

"It means you'll have to recruit two new suckers to do your dirty work," Devon retorted. "But there's two born every minute in Vegas, right?"

"But did Linda say where?" Pete asked, his face suddenly pale.

Devon rolled up a sweatshirt and shoved it into his bag. "No, she didn't. She only said she was sick of your lies. You made a fool of her, not that she didn't deserve it," he added cuttingly.

"You didn't tell her about, you know . . ." Pete paused, his eyes flashing with real fear now. "That the sappy stuff wasn't really from me?"

"It's all out in the open," Devon said. "Linda wasn't amused."

Pete rubbed his hands over his eyes and groaned. "And she didn't mention where she was going—how far?"

"All she said was 'home,'" Devon told him again.

"But I don't know where she's from!" Pete shouted, throwing up his hands. "How am I going to find her?"

"I don't think she wants you to find her," Devon said.

"Why did you tell her about those gifts?" Pete demanded. "Was that your way of getting back at me? She probably thinks I was just using her."

Devon raised his eyebrows. He was surprised to see that his uncle seemed more concerned about losing Linda than about the prospect of a jail sentence. "Drop the act! You *were* using her. Just like you were using me, *Uncle*."

"You're wrong there," Pete said. "I love Linda, I really do."

Devon let out a cruel laugh. "It's a little late to get all sappy about her now that she's gone, don't you think?"

Pete closed his eyes, shaking his head. "What have I done?" he mumbled woefully.

"I wouldn't worry about her, though," Devon continued. "Like you said, Linda is a classy girl. She'll probably forget all about you and find someone else by the end of the week."

Pete sucked in a quick breath, letting Devon know that his barb had hit its mark.

Devon finished packing and zipped up his bag. He flung his leather jacket over his shoulder and turned to go.

"Wait!" his uncle called.

Devon turned around and shot him a cold stare. "Wait for what?"

Pete's smooth veneer was completely gone now. His face was pale and drawn. He looked at Devon with a bleary-eyed expression that was etched with pain and despair.

"OK, I messed up with Linda," he said, pronouncing his words slowly, as if he was having difficulty speaking. "But I would still like you to stay."

A flutter of emotions squeezed Devon's throat.

He pushed them away, steeling himself against anything that might soften his resolve. "Forget it," he said. He grabbed his bag and walked out of the room.

Pete followed him to the front door of the apartment. "Devon, no matter what—we're family," he pleaded. "That part was never an act, kid."

Devon whirled around, his hand tightly gripping the doorknob. "Family?" he spat. "What a joke!"

With that, Devon walked out, slamming the door behind him. His stay in Vegas was over. He didn't know where he would go next, but the sooner he hit the open road, the better.

"Another miserable flop for the Wakefield duo," Jessica grumbled. It was Saturday night and she and Elizabeth were sitting side by side on the edge of the pool, dangling their feet in the water. "I can't believe how uncooperative Steven was today," Jessica added indignantly.

Elizabeth sighed. "I wasn't very comfortable lying to him all day about having to get the article done by Monday morning."

Jessica shook her head. "We already straightened that out, remember? You really might write about his internship, which automatically turns the lie into the truth."

Elizabeth gave her a withering look. "Your logic is amazing."

"Thanks," Jessica replied, even though she doubted her sister had meant it as a compliment. "I don't know why you always have to beat yourself up about things, Liz. You know what we're doing is right."

Elizabeth rolled her eyes. "I almost cracked up when you asked Steven to help you decide if law school was right for you."

"I can't believe he just brushed me off," Jessica grumbled. "This whole day has been one humiliating failure! I was so sure that hiding Steven's car keys would have made him late enough to infuriate Lila. And hinting to her that he'd driven back to SVU tonight should've pushed the girl completely over the edge."

Elizabeth leaned back, bracing herself with her elbows. "Hiding his car keys wouldn't have made a difference anyway," she stated calmly. "Steven keeps a spare set in his top drawer."

Jessica narrowed her eyes. "But he couldn't find them either," she said. Then she realized what must have happened to the second set of keys. "Elizabeth, you didn't!"

Elizabeth exhaled a very guilty-sounding sigh. "I feel absolutely terrible about it."

Jessica giggled. "You were one step ahead of me on that one. Very impressive!"

"But Steven is out with Lila, despite our efforts," Elizabeth pointed out. "I guess we have to come up with a better plan."

"I tried calling Billie today," Jessica said. "I wasn't able to reach her, but I left a dozen messages."

"What were you planning to say to her?" Elizabeth asked.

"I was going to tell her that Steven was miserable and wanted to meet her at the Palomar House for dinner to talk things out." Jessica smiled, pleased with her inspired creativity. "Too bad she never answered her phone."

Elizabeth glared at her. "Jessica, that would've caused a terrible scene!"

Jessica shrugged. "The subtle approach isn't working, in case you haven't noticed."

"I know," Elizabeth agreed. "Steven and Lila only seem to be getting closer."

Jessica kicked up a splash of water. "They're probably having a wonderful, romantic time right now. I can just see Lila batting her eyelashes at Steven . . . gushing over every word he says. How distasteful!"

"I don't know if getting Billie involved is the best move," Elizabeth said. "If she sees Steven with Lila, she might be so hurt and angry that she'll never want to get back together with him."

Jessica considered the possibility that Billie might not be the kind of girl who enjoyed competing over a guy. "I guess we're on our own," Jessica said, hooking her arm over her twin's shoulder. "We'll put our heads together—and this time, we'll come up with a plan that's totally foolproof!"

Lila groped her way through the crowded corridor in the Palomar House. Sirens were blaring, people were screaming. Everyone was soaking wet. *This is a nightmare!* she thought.

Suddenly, two strong arms reached for her. Lila turned and saw it was Steven. "Thank goodness," she cried with relief. She clung to him, unconcerned that his suit was drenched.

Finally, they stumbled through the exit. "What's going on?" Lila asked Steven. "Did a water hose break or something?"

Steven pushed his damp hair back and wiped his hand on his equally damp jacket. "It was the fire sprinklers," he told her.

The parking lot was teeming with police cruisers, an ambulance, and a fire truck. Lights were flashing, and bursts of static sounded from two-way radios. The fire had been extinguished before it had gotten out of hand. According to the bits of information Steven had overheard, the sprinklers had caused more damage than the fire itself. And despite the presence of an ambulance, no one had been seriously hurt.

Huddled together on a grassy spot near the entrance, Steven told her what he'd seen. "It was probably a homemade bomb," he said. "Someone just flung it through the window. It crashed to the floor and exploded into flames."

Lila began shaking. "Another deliberate fire."

Steven tightened his arms around her. "It's OK now," he said soothingly. "Let's go home."

Lila nodded, tears slipping down her face. But as they headed toward her car, they saw it was being checked out by a team of police officers. "What are they doing?" Lila whispered, looking to Steven for reassurance. It didn't appear as if they were examining any of the other cars in the parking lot.

Suddenly, more officers approached her and Steven. "Excuse me. Are you Lila Fowler, the registered owner of a green Triumph convertible?" He recited her license plate number.

Lila nodded mutely, her throat tightening as if she were being strangled.

"We'd like to escort you to police headquarters," the officer told her. But the hard look in his eyes contradicted the polite wording of his request. Lila wasn't fooled. *I'm in deep trouble,* she realized.

"What's going on?" Steven demanded.

The police officer turned to him. "What is your name, sir?"

"Steven Wakefield," he answered. "I was in the restaurant when the explosion occurred."

The officer wrote something in his small notepad. "Well, Mr. Wakefield, we're bringing Ms. Fowler in for questioning in regard to some items that have been discovered in her car."

Bewildered, Lila turned to Steven. "What are they saying?" she asked.

The police officer stepped closer to her. "Ms. Fowler, we'd really appreciate your cooperation. But an arrest warrant can be issued."

Lila blanched. "Arrest warrant?" she gasped.

"On what charges?" Steven asked. "What did you find in her car?"

"An empty container of nitrate fertilizer, traces of fuel oil in the upholstery, along with a few other flammable liquids, and a torn label fragment from a box of blasting caps," the police officer told them. "Your basic homemade fire-bomb paraphernalia."

"That's ridiculous!" Lila spat. "I don't know the first thing about firebombs or fertilizer!"

The officer gave her a cold stare. "These items were found in your car," he pointed out.

"I don't know how they got there!" Lila cried. "Someone else must've put them in my car. Tell them, Steven! Tell them I'm being set up again."

Steven put his arm around her. "Lila didn't do it," he said. "We were in the restaurant together."

"You're saying she was seated with you in the restaurant when the firebomb crashed through the window?" the police officer asked Steven.

Steven gripped her shoulder and said nothing. The police officer narrowed his eyes in a questioning look and tapped his pencil on his notebook.

"Not at the exact moment of the explosion," Steven answered finally. "Lila had gotten up to go to the ladies' room shortly before it happened."

The police officer slipped his notebook into his pocket. "OK, I've heard enough. We'll sort out the details at the station."

Lila stepped back. "I won't go!"

The police officer calmly took a set of handcuffs out of his pocket and slapped them on her wrists. "Lila Fowler, I'm placing you under arrest. . . ."

"This is a setup!" Lila screamed. "I didn't do it! I'm innocent!"

They pushed her into the back of a patrol car and slammed the door shut. *This is it*, Lila told herself, shaking uncontrollably. *They're going to lock me up forever, for a crime I didn't commit!*

Steven, her parents, her friends—none of them had been able to protect her from this terrifying ordeal. *I'm totally alone*, she thought, sobbing.

Steven stood in the parking lot of the Palomar House, shivering in his damp clothes, as he watched the patrol car drive away. *Don't worry, Lila*, he thought, hoping to send her a silent message of reassurance. *I'm going to get you out of this*.

Steven began to mentally click off what he needed to do to help Lila. *Get her a lawyer* . . . *post bail* . . . He thought about his father. Mr. Wakefield was a lawyer with a local firm and would definitely come through for Lila if Steven asked him. But the Fowlers probably had their own lawyers. Steven wondered if he should try reaching someone in the legal department of Fowler Industries instead of his father.

Steven headed back toward the restaurant

to find a phone. But as he made his way through the crowd of police officers, reporters, witnesses, and spectators, he kept hearing Lila's name being mentioned. He figured the story would soon be splashed all over the news, and that everyone would presume Lila was guilty.

Steven gritted his teeth, his fists clenched at his sides. *Lila is innocent!* he thought fiercely.

But deep inside, Steven felt a tiny spark of doubt. Lila hadn't been in the room when the firebomb crashed through the window. He couldn't remember how long she'd been gone before the explosion occurred. *A few minutes?* he asked himself silently. *Or longer—enough time to run outside, grab a bomb out of her car, and fling it through the window?*

Steven groaned softly. He hated himself for even thinking Lila capable of such a horrendous act of destruction. People could have been hurt, property had been damaged. He refused to believe Lila had been responsible.

All of a sudden John Pfeifer's dire warning came back to Steven, haunting him. "Lila is the type of girl who destroys anyone who cares about her," John had said. Steven had dismissed his ranting, presuming it was the lies of a violent criminal.

But what if Pfeifer was telling the truth? Steven wondered. *Will I be the next one on Lila's list?*

BANTAM BOOKS TEMPT YOU TO TURN BACK TIME AND
DISCOVER A SECRET SIDE TO THE WAKEFIELD TWINS,
THE TRUTH! NEVER COMPLETELY KNOWN BEFORE –
UNTIL NOW!

SWEET VALLEY HIGH™

created by Francine Pascal

JESSICA'S SECRET DIARY

Jessica . . . the untold story

Dear Diary,
     I'm leaving home. I can't stand it anymore. Elizabeth
stole the man I love. I've lost everything to her. I hate being a
twin. I hate always being compared to perfect Elizabeth.
     Only you know, Diary, just how much she's taken from
me. After tonight, I'm sorry I went behind Elizabeth's back with
Jeffrey French. I'm not sorry about any of the things I did to her.
     Good-bye, Sweet Valley. From now on Jessica
Wakefield is going to be one of a kind!

Read all about Jessica's agonizing dilemma in this special edition
featuring classic moments from Sweet Valley High™ books 30 to 40.

The first volume of Jessica's tantalizing secret diaries.

ISBN: 0-553-40866-6

FANCY A PRIVATE GLIMPSE INTO THE DIARY OF
ANOTHER? READ ON . . .

SWEET VALLEY HIGH™

created by Francine Pascal

ELIZABETH'S SECRET DIARY

Elizabeth . . . the untold story

Dear Diary,

  Todd and I are finished! I've never been more
miserable in my life. It all started when I found a letter on his
desk from a girl in Vermont. It sounded more than friendly, if you
know what I mean. I should trust Todd, but he didn't make things
better by getting mad at me for being a snoop (as he put it).

  I know what you're thinking, Diary. I have no right to
complain. When Todd was gone, I let Nicholas Morrow kiss me. I
even fell in love with Jeffrey French. But Todd doesn't know the
worst. Only you, Diary, know the true story of what happened
between Todd's best friend, Ken Matthews, and me.

Read all about Elizabeth's steamy affair in this special edition
featuring classic moments from Sweet Valley High™ books 20 to 30.

The first volume of Elizabeth's tantalizing secret diaries.

ISBN: 0-553-40927-1

All Transworld titles are available by post from:

Bookservice by Post, PO Box 29,
Douglas, Isle of Man IM99 1BQ

Credit Cards accepted.
Please telephone 01624 675137,
fax 01624 670923
or Internet http://www.bookpost.co.uk
or e-mail: bookshop@enterprise.net for details

Free postage and packing in the UK.
Overseas customers allow £1 per book (paperbacks)
and £3 per book (hardbacks).